MERMAID TEARS

MERMAID TEARS

SUSAN L. READ

IZZARD INK
PUBLISHING

IZZARD INK PUBLISHING
PO Box 522251
Salt Lake City, Utah 84152
www.izzardink.com

LIBRARY OF CONGRESS CONTROL NUMBER: 2020930533

Designed by: Alissa Theodor
Cover Design by: Andrea Ho
Cover Images: Shutterstock.com/Alenka Karabanova

First Edition

Contact the author at www.susanlread.com

Paperback ISBN: 978-1-64228-036-4

eBook ISBN: 978-1-64228-037-1

DEDICATED TO THE MEMORY OF
STEVE M. COHEN
WHO TAUGHT ME THAT "NORMAL" HAS NO MEANING.

AND TO ABBY
WHO BROUGHT SUCH PLEASURE WITH
WONDERFUL BOOK DISCUSSIONS.

Metamorphosis
of a Mermaid Tear

Ejected from the Earth.

Weathered

by wind, rain, time.

Dormant for millennia.

The crashing of the ocean waves

my only companion.

Soothed

by the rhythmic pulse,

the ambient sounds

of my never-resting friend.

Witness to

the beginnings of life.

Evolution

and natural selection

creating my new playmates.

Then the machines came,

shattering my peace

and my world.

Bulldozers loaded

billions and billions of us.

Trucks took us away.

Forged in fire.

Three thousand degrees Fahrenheit.

Poured into a mold.

Shaped.

Solid.

Transparent.

Now I can hold things.

Blackberry jelly

gives me a new purpose.

Proud to protect this treasure.

Crop after crop.

Year after year.

A favorite of this family.
Passed down,
mother to daughter.

But I am not immortal.
A cracked jar cannot be sterilized.
A new purpose.
Carrying candy
in a picnic basket.
Today's excursion
takes me back
to an old location.
A fun beach day.
Watching the children.

Then they dropped me.
Shattering me to pieces.
Abandoned now.
Useless.

Dormant for years.
The crashing of the ocean waves
my only companion.

Content.
Soothed by the rhythmic pulse,
the ambient sounds
of my never-resting friend.

Witness to
the extreme power of a hurricane.
Swept out to sea.
Worn by waves.
Recycled by the sea.

Ejected from the ocean.
Abandoned.
Useless.
Dormant.

Then a family came.
Adults under their sun umbrella.
Calling to the children.
"Sarah, Adam, Daniel,
it's time for lunch!"

Surprised, later that day,

to be plucked from the shore.

"You are beautiful!"

she cried.

"I am going to put you in my bottle

of mermaid tears.

I am going to keep you

forever!"

PART ONE

"From birth, man carries the weight of gravity on his shoulders. He is bolted to the earth. But man has only to sink beneath the surface and he is free."

- Jacques Cousteau

Why is it so hard
to be like other people?
Why is it so hard
to be normal?
Perhaps it would be better
if I wasn't even here.

Summer.

It's almost over.

Why does it always go by

so quickly?

School.

It hangs over me.

Like a giant storm cloud.

All summer long.

School.

I love learning.

I love routine.

I love organization.

So why can't I get my brain

to cooperate?

Why can't I focus for long enough

to make my teachers know

I am doing my best?

Why can't I seem to avoid

being labeled with words like:

immature,

disruptive,

inconsistent effort,

doesn't work well with others.

Why can't I get anything other than

that dreaded letter

C

on my report card?

Why can't I get my parents to understand

that I really am trying my best,

and that it is getting harder

and harder

to even keep earning that C?

I found out I needed glasses last year.

I found out that others did not see life

as a blur.

I thought that would help.

I can see the leaves on the trees now.

But I still can't control my brain.

Every year, teachers say things like,

"A new school year is like a new start.

Take advantage of it, Sarah!"

But how is it a new start when it's the same kids,

the same teachers,

the same building?

ONE

I CAN'T BELIEVE MY ELEMENTARY years are almost over. That's probably why this year seems to be going by rather quickly. More quickly than I want it to. We'll go back after April break, we'll do the dreaded MCAS tests, and it will be almost summer.

In many ways I will miss elementary school. Adams Elementary is such an interesting building, even though I know the teachers are all looking forward to the new one, which will be ready in a couple of years. Our school was built during the early years of the Cold War era, and it has a fallout shelter in the basement. There's still a sign outside the main office announcing its location.

Although the shelter was never used for its intended purpose, it is very well used now as a place to store broken furniture and teachers' junk. I've heard the custodian saying many times that it's not a storage place for things that belong in a dumpster, but I know that every year teachers send more and more of their belongings down there. Sometimes kids sneak down there, too, just to explore. But that's too creepy for me, so I've never ventured down in the six years I have been at the school.

Change is always scary, but maybe a change is what I need. There's no doubt that the past year or so has been getting more and more difficult for me, especially at school. Art class was always my escape. I used to really enjoy expressing myself through art. Used to. Until that art lesson last week, which changed everything for me.

We were working on sketching a still life in art class that day. There was a different arrangement of objects on each table, and we were allowed to choose which table to sit at. I chose the one that had the pine cones, a flower, and a large, beautiful seashell. I couldn't take my eyes off the shell. I was fascinated by its colors, its shape, and its shiny surface.

I started drawing, first the outline of the whole shell, then slowly adding the details. Fine lines. Shading. Texture. I worked carefully, putting all of my effort and concentration into this masterpiece.

Towards the end of the period, Mr. Miller asked us to put down our pencils. "It's time for our gallery walk," he announced.

Every art lesson with Mr. Miller ends the same way. We leave our work on our table and walk around the room, checking out our classmates' interpretations of the topic. I was so proud of my shell, and equally impressed by most of the other drawings. You could tell everyone was really focused, because the class had been much quieter than usual. At the end of our gallery walk, we collected our work to put in our portfolios.

As I was placing my shell carefully between the cardboard covers of my portfolio, admiring it one more time and hoping it would be selected for the school art show next month, Mr. Miller came over to me.

"I'm very disappointed in your effort today, Sarah," he said. Not quietly. "You usually seem to work quite hard in my class. I know you struggle with some other classes, and I guess I'm seeing that in here now. I noticed that you didn't even get close to finishing. There are no pine cones, and no flower. Everyone else managed to finish. I see no reason why you shouldn't have been able to!"

I didn't say anything. I've learned there is no point in trying to justify myself. Or my work. Or my behavior. Instead, I put on a mask. Make sure it is on firmly. No slipping. It would be there, firmly in place, for the rest of the year. And as we put our portfolios back on the shelf at the end of the lesson, I slipped that shell picture out and tore it up into tiny pieces. As I left the room, I threw them in the trash and checked again that my mask was in place.

I've always been fascinated by masks, especially the fancy ones you see people from other countries wear during cultural events. They can be so colorful and festive, decorated with feathers and beads and many different colors. They can be fun, but they can also evoke fear, especially when they are worn by warriors in their pre-battle rituals.

Masks can also be for protection from hazards in the environment. I remember reading a book last year about the first man to climb Mt. Everest - Sir Edmund Hillary. Climbing mountains was just what he did in his spare time. His full-time job was looking after 1,400 beehives with his brother as part of the family beekeeping business in Tuakau, New Zealand. The pictures in the book showed him in his beekeeping outfit, complete with full head mask, to protect him from bee stings. He also wore a mask when he climbed Mt. Everest. This mask was to deliver oxygen when he needed it, to protect him from the low-oxygen environment at the top of the mountain.

Wearing a mask at Halloween can be fun. Although we have always been encouraged to wear our costumes to school for classroom Halloween celebrations, we have never been allowed masks, make-up, or weapons. I like dressing up, and my costumes have never included any of those things.

Last year, I was Mary Poppins. My family and I had watched the movie a couple of weeks before Halloween. My grandmother told us that it was the first movie she ever saw in a movie theater. She remembered being fascinated by the special effects, especially how the characters climbed into the clouds. We all laughed about that, thinking about all the computer-generated special effects we have become used to on TV and in movies. I enjoyed it so much that I spent all of my spare time putting together an outfit. That's the kind of costume I like to wear: one I have made myself, with my mom's help. One that is not scary. My brothers prefer to buy theirs, and they believe that the more gruesome the costume is, the better. They usually have masks dripping blood and large, scary-looking weapons. Definitely not my style!

The really fun masks are the virtual reality ones. Earlier this year, the school purchased a class set of these, and it was awesome trying them out for the first time. Our teacher programmed several virtual field trips, and off we went without the need for those awful long bus rides, where so often someone gets sick. Never me, thank goodness.

Over the last few months, we have been on several of these "trips." My favorites so far have been the Amazon rainforest, the moon, and under the ocean. Virtual reality masks are just amazing. They allow you to enter into a completely different reality from the one you are living in. Even if it is only briefly, you are transported into another world. And you get to pick where you want to be! I wish I could have a virtual reality mask for my life. Then I wouldn't be so hurt by Mr. Miller's reaction to my art. Off I could go - to the Museum of Fine Art in Boston, or the Metropolitan Museum of Art in New York, or even one of the amazing art museums in Paris I have read about online. I could program my virtual world to have *my* art on the museum walls. I would be able to see members of the public walking around the museums admiring my work. Marveling at my skill. My use of color. My ability to show light and dark.

I want to live in that virtual world.

What is a mask?

Something to cover your face.

Protection.

Showing the world

only the parts

you want it to see.

What are the masks you hide behind?

Why?

What is it about you that you don't want

the world to see?

What do you think will happen

if the world

sees beneath your mask?

What do you do when you feel the mask

slipping?

Does it make you think

maybe it is time to discard the mask?

Or does it cause you to panic?

Cover it with another,

and another

and another

and another.

TWO

WE ARE A SCOUTING FAMILY. My parents were both Scouts when they were younger. My brothers are in the Boy Scouts and I'm in the Girl Scouts. My mother earned the Bronze, Silver, and Gold awards when she was a Girl Scout, so it feels like there is a lot of pressure on us kids to live up to the family reputation. I have always enjoyed creating things, and most of the badges I have earned so far are for creative activities. I feel really proud of myself when Mom sews another badge on my sash.

The badges I have had the most fun with, so far, anyway, are drawing, gardening, and digital photography. I have a little spot behind the garage that is my garden. I enjoy researching what will grow best there and arranging the plants in different ways. I even made an edging around the garden with some rocks and a few of the biggest shells from my collection. My garden has even been the subject of some of my drawings and photos. I like drawing it, or photographing it, at different times of the day to see the light and the shadows in different places.

Our family also likes to go geocaching together when the weather is nice, so it was really a family achievement when I earned my geocaching badge. Mom actually showed me how to do tiny stitches and sew my own badges when I got that one. I feel doubly proud of my sash now.

Geocaching is when you use a handheld GPS or an app on your phone to find a container that someone has hidden. They post the coordinates for what they have hidden on a website, and when you find it, you sign a log-book in the container and add a note to the cache page on the web site. Sometimes the container you find is big enough to hold little trade items. When we find one like that, I always leave a little plastic frog, and choose something to take in exchange. Most of the caches we have found have been in lovely peaceful natural settings, like in the woods, or by a stream, or in a park. I love being outside. In nature. Nature doesn't judge. Nature doesn't have unrealistic expectations or tell me how disappointed it is. Nature is a place to be at peace. Nature inspires me.

Geocaching has been around for a while, even before I was born, but my parents didn't start until a few years ago when a friend of Mom's told her about it. I have heard Mom and Dad talk many times about how they think we do not spend enough time doing things together as a family. I know they both work long hours, especially Dad, who often gets called into work on the weekends, which makes Mom really mad. I am sure that was a big part of the reason why, when they learned about it, they decided it would be a good thing to try. Mom's friend Wendy and her husband, Tom, have been geocaching for many years and have found over seven thousand. We have found 556 so far. It's fun, and has taken us to some really interesting places that Mom and Dad say they would never have found on their own.

We found two caches for my geocaching badge, and I think they are the most interesting ones we have found so far. The first one was in Randolph, Massachusetts. The cache was at the site of an old abandoned Nike missile site, left-over from the Cold War. We parked at the bottom of a hill and climbed what looked to be a long, deserted road to the top. I wasn't really sure what I expected to see there, but I know I was not expecting what we found. Before we even went searching for the cache, we examined the many abandoned buildings, covered now with vines and graffiti. On some of the buildings, nature was winning, but on many of them were an assortment of pictures and words that made Mom and Dad question whether this was a good place to bring the family! I was fascinated to think that this place had once been home to missiles, ready to fire if our country was threatened. When I got home, I got out my iPad and looked up Nike missile bases so I could learn more about their history.

The second one was a really fun cache, although very different from the missile base. It was in the woods in Needham, Massachusetts. To get to the cache site, you had to follow a trail that was marked by miniature birdhouses attached to the trees. The roof color of each birdhouse indicated which trail you were following, and if you followed the correct colors, you came to an absolutely amazing miniature railway in a small clearing in the woods.

The owner of the cache lives nearby, and he loves to come out and demonstrate the workings of the trains. We had signed the log-book and were just about to leave when he came over. He must have heard all the noise Adam and Daniel were making. For once, having noisy brothers was a good thing! We told him that this was our family's one hundredth geocache find and that I was earning my Girl Scout geocaching badge for finding it. He sounded really happy that his cache was the one we had chosen for both of these special occasions.

He got the train working for us and then invited us all to his house where his wife made us hot chocolate while he showed us his workshop, where he makes the miniature birdhouses and pieces for his railway. Adam and Daniel were fascinated with all the train stuff and asked him lots of questions, like how he made sure the tracks didn't wear out over the winter, but I was more interested in the process of turning plastic tubing into those exquisite, tiny bird-houses, and I was so excited when he gave me one to keep! He even let me choose which roof color I would like. I chose green, because Signal the Frog is the mascot of geocaching, and I have a Signal soft toy that I always take on caching adventures. One day when I have my own house and garden, I might hang it from one of my trees, but for now it has a special place on my bookcase.

Sometimes we earn badges by ourselves, and sometimes we work on them together with other troop members. Last summer, our troop leader told us that we were going to work together to earn our camping badge. We have been working on it in stages, and this weekend will be the final part. We are going camping, and we will, hopefully, all come home with our camping badges.

This time it will be a little different from previous camps. In other camps, we have always shared a big tent with other girls, usually six or eight in a tent. I don't like being crowded together like that. But this time we can choose to either share a big tent with others, or we can take a small tent, if we have one, and set up our own individual camp alongside the others. That kind of sounds like fun.

I talked to Dad, because he has a small tent he sometimes uses when he goes on hunting or fishing trips with his friends. He said I was welcome to use it, as long as I was careful with it, so we have spent time practicing pitching it in the backyard. I have even slept in it a few times to get used to it. What can go wrong?

After my parents drive me to the campsite, there is the usual: "Ask Mrs. Bryan to call us if there is any problem" (Mrs. Bryan is our Troop Leader, and the only one allowed to bring a phone to camp), "Remember to be careful about nuts," (I have a nut allergy. Seriously, how old am I? I think I can remember not to eat nuts.), and "Have fun!"

As soon as all the parents leave we start to set up our campsite. About half of the girls are going to be sharing tents. It takes quite a few people to get one of those tents set up, so they all work together on one, and then the next, until all of their tents are ready. The rest of us get together and plan out where we will each pitch our tents. Surprisingly, there's not a lot of disagreement about who should go where. Everyone picks a spot, and everyone else seems happy with their choices. Mine is going to be on the side, almost underneath a lovely oak tree. We're all quite excited about being much more independent than usual at camp, so there's a lot of talking and giggling going on as we get ourselves all set up for the weekend.

I have practiced so many times that I have no difficulty at all getting my tent ready to go. I can tell some of the others don't really know what they are doing though, so we all help each other once we are done with our own tents. Once all our tents are pitched, our beds unrolled, and our bags inside, the "little-tent campers," as we are calling ourselves, gather around and share stories of our April break adventures so far. One girl, Helen, tells us that her family went to Disney World for several days. She took the last week out of school, which makes us all jealous, but then she tells us that there was a heat wave in Florida at the time. She tells us how they spent most of their time there going on rides that were inside to enjoy the air-conditioning. The rest of us are kind of envious about Disney World, but not about the heat wave!

I think my favorite part of any camp is after dinner. We cook our meal over an open fire, then build the fire up, gather round, and sing silly campfire songs. As we get tired, we are free to drift off to our sleeping bags and settle in for the night. I have packed my book and my flashlight, so I am planning on an early night followed by lots of reading. At home, Dad will often come by my room and tell me it is time to turn out the light and go to sleep if I am reading for "too long," so I am looking forward to having no deadline here at camp. We sing a few songs, and off I go. It's too hot to get into my sleeping bag, so I settle on top of it, get out my flashlight and book, and start reading. I can hear the singing getting quieter and quieter as others drift off to bed.

One of the reasons I didn't enjoy shared tent camping was the noise. The others would want to talk and giggle until well into the night. I have found that if I don't spend some time being quiet, I have a lot of difficulty getting to sleep. As the night wears on, I can hear the noise from the big tents, and some of the little tent girls are obviously visiting their neighbors, but from my position on the edge under the oak tree, it is not so loud that I can't tune it out and focus on my book. At some point I guess I drift off to sleep. I wake up at first light on Saturday to find my flashlight still turned on and my book discarded beside my sleeping bag.

For this camp, we are focusing on outdoor crafts and skills, so after breakfast, we have a chance to do some horseback riding, which is great fun. We are camping right next to a place that does a riding camp for the disabled every summer, so we take advantage of our neighbors being horses. The owner came to several of our troop meetings back home before camp started to teach us about caring for horses. He showed us how to tack up the horses, and we all get a chance to show off what we have learned on the wooden horses while we wait to ride.

Riding the horses is amazing. The horses are very well trained so that none of the disabled people who take part in their programs will get hurt in any way, so we all know we are perfectly safe. Mr. James, the owner, leads us on a long, gentle walk over the hilly area of his stable and gives us a little history lesson on the area as we ride. None of us girls really say very much. I can tell from the looks on everyone's faces that they are as focused on enjoying both the horses and the history as I am.

When we have finished our ride, Mr. James quizzes us about what he taught us during our troop meetings. Just before lunch, he and Mrs. Bryan together present us all with our horseback riding badges. Everyone rushes off to their tents to put their badges away. We have worked too hard on these to risk losing them. I tuck mine carefully away in my bag. I look forward to sewing it onto my sash when I get home.

To earn our camping badge, we have to master quite a few camping and outdoor skills. Two of the things

Mrs. Bryan told us we have to be able to do without adult assistance are to pitch our tents and set up the camp-site. Before camp, we were divided into groups. Each group would be responsible for the planning and cooking of one meal for all of the campers. We had to stick to a budget and show that we were providing a healthy meal. We would need to be able to build and light a fire (without using paper to get it going) and use a map to find our way around the area where we are camping.

My group is responsible for Saturday lunch. Janet, Helen, Erin, Abby, and Julia are all in my group. When we met before camp to do our planning, we decided to serve chicken sausages (we checked first that there were no vegetarians) with a salad and bread rolls, lemonade to drink, and cookies for dessert. We checked with Mrs. Bryan to see if it was okay to bring cookies we had made at home, and she said yes, as long as the rest of the meal is made at camp. Of course the bread rolls won't be exactly made at camp, although we are going to heat them on our fire before we serve them. We all agreed when we were planning the meal that heated rolls are the best!

Janet has proven herself to be a wonderful cookie maker on many occasions. She loves to try out new recipes and will often bring some to our troop meetings to get our opinion on whether she should make that recipe again. We always say yes! So, by unanimous vote, Janet is our cookie maker for the weekend. The rest of us set about creating lunch for the campers, as well as Mr. James who has been invited to join us.

First up - fire lighting. Julia arranges the kindling wood that we all gathered and strikes one of our two matches. Success! She doesn't even have to use the second match, let alone ask Mrs. Bryan for more. It's a great start. Soon she is able to begin feeding bigger pieces onto the fire, and before very long at all, it looks ready for us to begin cooking the sausages. Abby is in charge of not burning the sausages while Julia keeps the fire going. That leaves Helen, Erin, and me to make the salad and wrap the rolls in foil to heat a little just before lunch is served.

"Who wants to chop what?" Helen asks us.

"I'd like to do the tomatoes, please," I reply. "My grandmother showed me a great way of cutting them into flower shapes. I'd like to do those for everyone."

Helen and Erin sound pleased with that idea, so I start chopping. That leaves lettuce, cucumbers, baby carrots (which don't need chopping – we are putting them in the salad whole), and radishes. Helen and Erin work on those. While the sausages are cooking, Abby and Julia also set up the tablecloth, plates and cups, salad dressings, and lemonade. Finally we remove the rolls from the fire, and our meal is ready to serve. My little group receives many compliments on our efforts. It makes me feel really good inside when I hear people commenting on the flower tomatoes.

We work through one skill after another and are rewarded after dinner with the presentation of our camping badges. Mine joins my horseback riding badge, carefully placed in a pocket in my bag. I am really excited to earn two new badges in one day! I can't wait to get that sash out when I get home.

After dinner, Mrs. Bryan tells us she is proud of all our hard work during the day and that she has some fun games planned for us during campfire time. She brings out a huge box of glow sticks. The first game is glow stick hide and seek. Once it gets dark, we snap the glow sticks and each put one of the long ones around our necks, like a collar. There's an orange team and a blue team. We divide ourselves into two groups pretty easily. It's just for fun, so groups of friends join together. I'm on the orange team, along with Erin and Julia, as well as a bunch of other girls.

We take turns to hide, with the other team trying to find us without flashlights. We're not allowed to cover our glowing necks. Some girls are really good at hiding and take quite some time to find. I get found quickly, so I head on over to the campfire to join the others from orange team who have already been found. Mrs. Bryan times the teams to see which one finds all of their opposition in the shortest amount of time. Orange team wins!

By now, it is really dark because we have let the campfire die down. We play glow stick tic-tac-toe. It is just like regular tic-tac-toe but with glow sticks making the grid, and the *Os* and *Xs*. We keep switching partners after each game, playing until the campfire is completely extinguished. After a cup of hot chocolate, it is time for bed.

By the time I get back to my tent, I am completely exhausted. It's been a very long and busy day, with so many activities and achievements that my brain is having a major disagreement with the rest of me. My body needs sleep, but my mind is racing. My brain is jumping from one thought to another. Eventually my body joins in. I can't keep still. My tent can no longer contain my energy. It spills out. I decide to take a walk to calm myself down. The talking and giggling from the other tents has died down, and I don't want to disturb anyone, so I unzip my tent quietly and step outside.

I take my flashlight with me. My plan is to walk around the campsite for a while until I feel as though I can fall asleep. I walk. I walk. I walk. I walk. I walk. I walk. I walk.

As the sun starts to come up, I wonder where I am. I wonder what has happened. I wonder where I have come from. I wonder where I was going. I wonder what I should do. Before I can even begin to think, to make any decisions about what to do next, my confusion is interrupted by flashing blue lights and strong uniformed arms picking me up off the ground. Voices tell me everything will be all right. I can stop screaming now. They will take me back to camp, and my parents will be there to meet us. Everything is going to be all right. I can stop crying now. Everything is going to be all right.

I don't know how long it takes to get back to the campsite, and I don't know where it was that they found me. I don't know what they say to me in the car, and I don't know what they say to my parents when we arrive at camp. Somehow my tent gets packed up and put into the trunk of my parents' car. I don't know what they say on the way home. Once we arrive home, it is a different matter.

We all sit down around the dining room table. Dad keeps saying over and over again that they need to be sure they have my full attention. Mom is crying and saying she just does not understand. Finally, Dad asks the question. "Why?"

Why what? I don't understand what is wrong. I can't explain in my own head what happened, so how can I possibly explain to my parents? Dad tells me that Mrs. Bryan discovered my empty tent and called the police. Apparently, I was found several miles from the campsite, sitting by the side of the road, screaming and crying.

"What on earth were you thinking?" Dad asks. "Were you trying to run away?" When I don't answer, he continues with his questions.

"Did something happen at camp to make you act in such an irresponsible way?"

Still I don't answer, because he wants information that I cannot give him because I don't have it myself. Eventually, we all get tired of this fruitless meeting.

"I need to go and lie down," Mom says. I can't tell from the look on her face whether she is angry or upset with me. Probably both.

"Go upstairs," Dad tells me. "Do not come out of your room until I tell you to."

I go upstairs and tuck myself up in my bed. I run the events of the weekend over and over in my mind, trying to make some kind of sense out of what happened. I can't. It makes no sense.

I know that Saturday was a busy day. I know there was a lot happening and that when I went to bed, I was struggling to settle my thoughts and calm my body and mind and be ready for sleep. I know I decided to go for a little walk around the campsite, thinking it would help me get to sleep. How that turned into an all-night walk, with me ending up not knowing where I was and the police having to come out to search for me, is quite beyond my powers of reasoning. Mom and Dad told me how frantic Mrs. Bryan sounded on the phone when she called to say I was missing and that the police were searching for me. I know they were really worried about me too, and I certainly do owe them an explanation. But I can't give them one because I can't give myself one. I have no idea what happened.

I pull the covers more tightly around me and go over and over the events of the last twenty-four hours in my mind. Nothing like this has ever happened to me before. Lately, I have been feeling as though I have been losing control of myself at times, but nothing like this. Nothing like losing hours of my life. Nothing like finding myself in a completely unknown place. Nothing like putting this amount of stress and worry on people I care about.

Later in the afternoon, after I have picked at the sandwich Mom brought me for lunch, I unpack my camp bag. Mom comes into my room and sits on my bed. She isn't saying very much. I can tell she is hoping I will talk to her, but I just keep working on my bag. When I take my two new badges out of the pocket they were in, Mom gets up and goes downstairs. She returns a couple of minutes later with her sewing basket. She sits back down on my bed and quietly sews my new badges onto my sash. Neither of us says anything, but later, when she leaves my room, she gives me a hug.

Later, Dad knocks on my bedroom door and, without waiting for a response, comes into the room.

"It's dinner-time. You can come down now." That's all he says, before he heads back down the stairs. I'm nervous. Are Mom and Dad going to start up with the questions again? I hope not, because I still don't know what to say. Although Adam and Daniel both give me some strange looks as we sit down at the table, no-one says anything about camp.

Mom suggests I get an early night, since I obviously didn't sleep at all last night. That sounds like a good idea. I'm exhausted.

"Goodnight," I say as I head for the stairs. "I'm sorry. I really am."

Those words don't seem even close to enough, but I have no idea what else to say.

"Let's not talk about this anymore today," Mom says. "Just try to get a good night's sleep, and I'm sure we will all see things more clearly in the morning."

I don't think anything will be clearer in the morning. I lie in bed, wondering how I will turn my mind off. My thoughts drift to school tomorrow. In a strange way, I think I am actually looking forward to it. Anything to take my mind off this disaster of a weekend.

Careful.

Be careful.

Avoid people.

Be careful.

Don't be noticed.

Be careful.

Make them forget.

Be careful.

They are watching now.

Be careful.

Blend in.

Be careful.

Silence.

Be careful.

Compliance.

Be careful.

Be normal!

THREE

I DECIDE THE BEST THING I can do at school is to avoid people as much as possible. I manage to get through the day, barely speaking to anyone except the teachers. That's not too difficult to do, since I don't really have too many friends at school any-more. I used to. I do remember that when I was in the lower grades, I would look forward to seeing my friends at school and spending time with them after school and on the weekends. Those times would be spent happily in our imaginary worlds with our dolls. Building huts in the bushes behind my house. Secret clubs. Long bike rides. Great memories, but just memories now.

Patricia is about the only one I still hang out with regularly. We don't have the same lunch or recess times this year, though, so we don't see each other much at school. We do still spend a lot of time on the weekends doing things together, and she has even come with my family a few times when we have gone geocaching. She enjoyed that so much that she has got her own family interested enough to start doing it themselves.

Patricia and I enjoy playing with our dolls. Especially Barbie. We spend hours dreaming up imaginary lives for them, using our creative skills to make clothes, and even writing stories about their adventures. Sometimes at her house. Sometimes at mine. Occasionally we get together after school if there is not too much homework. This afternoon she is coming to my house. She lives just down the street, so we get off at the same bus stop. "See you soon!" she yells as she heads off for her own house to drop off her backpack and check in with her mother.

I walk into my own house to the delicious smell of chocolate chip cookies. My grandmother, who is a much better baker than my mother, always has a freshly made snack waiting for us after school. She comes over every day after school for an hour or two to supervise snacks, homework, and anything else that is going on. I love spending time with my grandmother. She used to be a nurse until she retired. She always tells us kids there is nothing we could possibly do that would shock her. She has seen it all, she says.

"Hi, Gran," I greet her as I give her the usual after-school hug. I'm sure she knows about what happened over the weekend, but she doesn't say anything as I take off my backpack and put my lunchbox on the kitchen counter.

"How was school today, sweetheart?"

"The usual." I'm sure she doesn't even know what the usual is, but she accepts my answer. Mom has already told her that Patricia is coming over this afternoon and that we are allowed to hang out together for an hour. Then I have to get to my homework. I'm actually a little surprised that I got permission to have this after-school time since my grades have been slipping a bit just lately. It's not that I am not working hard, but I'm pretty sure that is what my parents are thinking.

"Hi, Patricia," my grandmother greets her as she arrives. "You are just in time. The cookies are fresh out of the oven!"

The afternoon begins really well! Patricia chooses lemonade, but I prefer apple juice. We head into the dining room to enjoy my grandmother's baking skills. Once we have finished munching and chatting, we head upstairs to my room, where our adventures usually happen. I noticed when she arrived that she hadn't brought any of her dolls with her, but mine are all lined up on my bed, ready, and I am always happy to share.

"I thought we could do something different today," Patricia announces as we get into my room and she sees the dolls. "I really think we are both getting too old to still be playing with dolls. Maybe we could play cards? Or a video game? Or do some drawing?" she adds. Those are all things we enjoy doing together, but hearing her say those words has a strange effect on my brain.

"What do you mean we are too old?" I scream. A lot more words come out of my mouth too. I look at Patricia's face. She looks shocked. Horrified. Terrified of this stranger in front of her. Without a word, she walks out of my bedroom. Out of my house.

I sit down on my bed, trying to untangle in my mind what has just happened. I look across at my dolls and pick up the one named Patricia. I named her a long time ago after the friend I have always enjoyed spending time with. I wonder if she will ever want to get together again.

Explosion.

Violent.

Explosion.

Shattering.

Explosion.

Destructive.

Explosion.

Blowing apart.

Explosion.

Exactly what it feels like

inside my brain.

Out of control.

Calm one minute.

Destroy everything around me the next.

The shock waves

radiating outwards.

No end

to their destructive power.

Internal
and external
combustion.

FOUR

FOR A PERSON WHO DOESN'T enjoy the feel of salt water on her skin, I think my fascination with mermaids is kind of unusual. I'm not sure what it is about them that fascinates me the most. Their beauty. The way they glide effortlessly through the water. They are so graceful. (I am not graceful at all.) The fact that they are not real. I am wishing more and more just lately that I weren't real.

I have read a lot about mermaids, and they are my favorite thing to draw or paint. When I was learning to sew on buttons when I was a Junior Girl Scout, Mom took me to the craft store to choose some buttons. As we were walking toward the buttons aisle, I remember noticing a beautiful fleece fabric covered with mermaids. Suddenly I knew why I had been saving my allowance for so long! When I explained my idea to my mother, she said she was happy to pay for half of the fabric, as well as for the buttons. It took me many days, but I carefully sewed buttons on the tails of several of the mermaids, creating a blanket I was so proud of that it is still on my bed. I remember my leader being amazed. She had said we would pass the activity, and earn the achievement badge, if we could show her that we had sewn on four buttons!

I have even sewed a soft toy of a mermaid. My grandmother helped me with the tricky parts, like pushing the stuffing into the thin arms. I was really pleased with the way it turned out and proud of myself when Mom told me the finished doll was really impressive. I try hard to make Mom and Dad pleased with me, but it doesn't always work out. I feel as though Adam and Daniel get a lot more of their attention than I do. Maybe that's because they are always so loud. Or maybe it's because Mom and Dad are always having to drive them to sports events, while I'm usually just doing my own thing quietly in my room. But my grandmother notices me, and not because I get into trouble.

We spend a lot of time just talking about all kinds of things while we work on our crafts together. She tells me stories about how things were when she was my age, and we talk a lot about whether she would prefer to be a kid now or back then. She hasn't really reached a conclusion to that big question yet. I feel so grateful that my grandmother and I seem to understand each other so well, but I wish I knew how to have the same relationship with Mom and Dad.

I remember once reading a story about the ancient goddess Atargatis, who was one of the gods of the Assyrian
Empire, one of the great empires of the ancient Middle
East. The story told how she fell in love, but not with another god. She fell in love with a mortal man, a shepherd.
She was carrying his child, but these two did not get to
live a happy-ever-after life like the stories I like to write.
Atargatis accidentally caused him to drown, and because
of this, she had so much guilt that she tried to drown herself. But she was a goddess and could not die. Instead of
drowning, she was transformed into a beautiful mermaid.

I read a lot of books about mermaids, but this one particularly fascinated me, so I spent a lot of time trying to
find out more information about her. I found out that she
was connected to the constellation Pisces. That's my birth
sign. Maybe that's part of my fascination with her, and with
mermaids in general. I also found out some other connec-
tions to my own life. The Assyrian Empire apparently in-
vented longitude and latitude, which my family uses when
we go geocaching. They were also responsible for the di-
vision of a circle into three hundred and sixty degrees,
which is part of geometry, my favorite (or least hated) part
of math. I also read that they were the first to create an an-
tidepressant. Apparently patients would inhale the fumes,

which would help them to overcome the effects of sorrow or grief. I wonder if that would help me when I am feeling sad and struggling with parts of my life.

But ever since I read her story and learned that it was guilt that caused her transformation, I began to feel really strongly that mermaids and I have a deep connection.

The legend tells how Atargatis would help anyone who followed her to overcome their fears and dark thoughts and be able to develop a love for who they are inside. Inside me there is a lot of guilt, and a lot of fears and dark thoughts. But as time goes on, I am not sure that developing a love for who I am is something that is ever going to be possible.

Guilt is a very powerful thing. I have so much guilt inside of me right now. There's guilt about the the way my behavior is beginning to affect other people. I just don't know how to deal with it.

There's guilt about disappointing my parents. I know they both work so hard to provide us kids with what we need. I often wish they didn't work so hard, so that perhaps we could spend more time together and I would feel like I could go to them just to talk when something is bothering me. They work hard so we can have what we need, so why can't I give them what they need? A well-behaved, academically successful daughter. I don't understand some of my recent behavior, so I don't know what to do about it. I don't understand why, despite all my hard work, I just cannot seem to improve my grades.

There's guilt about the way I look. I know I am over-weight. I know I have a lot of pimples. I know my parents do not like either of those things. I've heard them talking many times about how I don't take care of myself properly. But they are wrong. I really do try to do all the right things. Sometimes I feel as though my skin is going to come off, I scrub so hard; but no matter what I do, the pimples re-main. I definitely wish they didn't. They are just one of the many things I get picked on about at school.

Guilt caused Atargatis to try to drown herself. Guilt causes me to want to hide from the world more and more often these days. If only that were possible.

I think a lot about the world of the mermaid. I think it would be absolutely magical to live underwater. All of the oceans of the world would be my playground. So much to explore. So much to challenge me. When an underwater documentary comes on television, I am transfixed. The beauty of the underwater plants is beyond words. It seems such a shame that they only grow underwater, where most of the people of the Earth will never get a chance to view their splendor. Thank goodness for underwater explorers and documentary crews.

When Dad was younger, he used to watch *"The Under-sea World of Jaques Cousteau"* on television. He has always enjoyed fishing, but he can't swim, so he has only ever been in a boat on the water. Never in the water or under it. Last year for Christmas, Mom bought him the complete DVD set of that series. He likes to play it over and over again, which is fine by me! I have even developed a love of the music of John Denver, who sang the beautiful theme song, "Calypso," from that series.

As well as the plant life under the ocean, I just love watching the amazing assortment of animal life that dwells beneath the waves. From the microscopic to the majestic humpback whale, the ocean contains so much more variety of life than I have seen on land. I know that more than half of the life on our planet is in the oceans, and I guess that makes a lot of sense when I look at the globe in the library at school and see how much of it is blue. I am sure they all have their own ways of communicating with each other, but when I am watching them on television, it seems like an almost noiseless and tranquil environment.

I know that I am oversimplifying what it would be like to live in the ocean. I know there are conflicts and dangers, but my vision of life for mermaids is one of quiet contentment. They are imaginary, so the life I design for them in my mind does not have to be based in any kind of reality. I often wish I were a mermaid, a mythical being of great beauty with the vastness of the world's oceans as my playground.

But the reality of my life right now is so different. I feel as though I am completely trapped in an ever-decreasing circle. After the camp weekend, I wanted to stop going to Girl Scouts, but both Mom and Dad keep saying I cannot let the family down like that. They want all their children to be members of the organization that was so important to them. We don't have to get all the badges they did, but we do have to do our best there.

I felt so awkward going to that first meeting after camp. No-one said anything to me about it, or questioned me, but I felt so uncomfortable knowing that everyone knew what had happened. Mrs. Bryan didn't treat me any differently from the way she had before camp, but it just didn't seem right to me that I was no more able to explain it all to her than I was to my parents. I hoped those feelings would go away eventually, but they didn't. They got worse. I have decided I just do not want to go any more. But how am I going to tell Mom and Dad?

It's Tuesday night. Troop meeting night. Usually I load the dishwasher after dinner, but on troop nights, Adam and Daniel do it. They are just about to start when I interrupt them.

"I'll do it." I start to clear the plates from the table.

"You can't do it," Mom interrupts me. "You'll be late for your meeting."

"I'm not going. I want to quit."

"What on earth are you talking about, Sarah?" Mom looks shocked, which kind of surprises me. After all, since that camp weekend, I've talked about not going back many times.

"Sarah, I'm sure it's difficult for you to go to the meetings with the other girls there all knowing about what happened at camp. But I'm pretty sure they've forgotten about it all by now. I'm sure they have all got things going on in their own lives to think about."

"Please, Mom," I beg. But she just shakes her head.

"No. I will not allow you to quit. Get your things together, and I'll drive you to the meeting."

So I go upstairs, get my sash and change my shoes, and prepare myself for another troop meeting.

It goes on like this for several more weeks. As each Tuesday night approaches, I tell Mom and Dad that I am not going to the meeting. They tell me that I am, and I end up going. Each week we argue about it more and more.

"I've had enough of this," Dad announces one Tuesday night after dinner. "If you want to quit that badly, you can quit. But I hope you know how disappointed we all are with your decision."

So it's part relief, and part more guilt. It's not much to ask, is it? To go to Girl Scout meetings and keep up the family tradition. But I just can't do it. I don't want to disappoint anyone, but going to the meetings just makes me think about camp. My once-treasured sash is folded up and put away in a drawer. Thankfully, none of my troop members are in my class at school, so I don't have to face them every day.

Today is shaping up to be a typical day at school. None of the kids really speak to me, except when it is necessary for work that we are doing in groups. I used to ask if I could work on my own, but the teachers would always say no. They would say that it was time I learned to work well with others and to behave in a more mature way. I don't understand what was immature about my behavior, I really don't. They would say that my academic record so far showed quite clearly that I was not capable of completing the assignment on my own. I would need to work with my peers. So I've stopped asking.

Lunch-time is, as usual, the worst part of the day. We all have assigned seats in the cafeteria. Each class has two tables, so you never have to wonder where you will sit, or if you will be sitting alone. Today, as has become usual, no-one speaks to me during lunch. I've actually been finding it more and more difficult to sit in the cafeteria for the twenty minutes of lunch-time. It feels like an increasingly noisy and hostile environment. A while ago I started asking to go to the nurse, claiming stomach pains, or to the bathroom. I would take my time coming back, walking as slowly as I could. I try that again today, but I guess I take too long to come back this time. As I walk back into the cafeteria, I hear a voice.

"Just sit down and eat your lunch like everyone else, Sarah!" the voice demands.

———

I'm sitting in my bedroom, staring at the homework that needs to be done and thinking back over the day. I guess I will not be using that lunch strategy again. The now-frequent question comes into my mind. Why can't I be like everyone else? Why can't I be normal? I don't know how to explain to myself, or to anyone else, that sometimes it feels like I become another person. Someone else jumps out of me, takes control, and tries her very best to sabotage my life.

If I really were a mermaid I would just swim away. I would find a new part of the ocean to hide myself in. But I'm not a mermaid. I'm just me. And that me is stuck here. Stuck in my life. Stuck in my house. Stuck in my bedroom. I try hard not to think of it as being stuck, but that's how I feel.

When I am feeling this way, I have developed a strategy to try to help myself cope. To feel unstuck. So I set to work. I look around my small bedroom. There's really only room for a bed, a chest of drawers, a small bedside table, a bookshelf that fits under the window, and a built-in closet. That's all. There's not much room to move things around, and there are definitely no combinations I have not tried many times before, but here I go. Bed over here. Drawers over there. I can't move the bookcase, because Dad made it to fit under the windows, so it's stuck, like me. I can't move the closet either, and I am not allowed to hang up posters. Dad always says, "When you have your own house, you can hang up as many posters as you like, but no holes in my walls!" so I try to decorate by laying my mermaid drawings all over the surfaces of the furniture. Mom doesn't like that idea. She says it looks messy, so I just keep my door shut.

After I move the furniture, I put away all the drawings that have been out and replace them with a whole new set. I look around my room once I have finished. It does look a little different than it did when I left for school this morning. But I am still stuck.

***

I always thought of mermaids as being happy and content with their lives. Their beauty and their freedom would certainly make me happy. Then I learned that sea glass, which I love to collect, is sometimes known as mermaid tears. That really got me thinking about what would make a mermaid cry. Perhaps loneliness? Perhaps fear of the unknown? Perhaps fear of rejection? Perhaps the disbelief of others? There's another reason I wish I were a mermaid. The salt water of the ocean would wash the tears away. Just like wearing a mask, so no-one would know. I could really use that kind of mask.

FIVE

FOR THE REST OF THE school year, I have to ride to school on the school bus, trying to ignore the presence of my former friend Patricia. I've tried to apologize to her. I've tried to explain that my behavior wasn't directed at her, and that I really want us to be friends again. But she has made it very clear she is not interested. Not even a little bit. Eventually I am forced to accept that she has made up her mind and has no intention of changing it.

Now school is finally over for the year. Fifth grade is over. Adams Elementary is over. Big changes are coming. But for the next two months, I am going to try very hard to forget all that. I am going to try very hard to forget that I don't have my friend to invite over for all the things we used to enjoy doing together. I am going to try to forget that I won't be asking that friend to join us on our geocaching adventures.

I'm going to read. I'm going to draw. I'm going to go on long bike rides, as long as it isn't too hot. I'm going to hang out in the back yard under the apple tree. I'm going to count down the days until we go for our annual vacation week to Dennis.

It seems like the summer is never going to end. I'm trying to get through the days. I'm trying to wait patiently for Dennis. I'm glad that Patricia's family has gone away for a month-long vacation to Texas to visit her grandparents. I heard her talking about it at lunch the last week of school, and I felt so relieved that I wouldn't have to keep making excuses to Mom about why I wasn't inviting her over. I think my best coping strategy to get through the summer is books.

Last summer I got to meet the author of a series I enjoyed reading in fourth grade. Victoria J. Coe wrote the Fenway and Hattie series, about a girl and her dog. The thing I really liked about the books is that they are told from the dog's point of view, which leads to all sorts of hilarious misunderstandings. Reading those books made my longing for a dog even stronger.

When Mom showed me on Facebook that Victoria J. Coe was going to be appearing at the Blue Bunny Bookshop in Dedham, I knew I wanted to go and meet her. At that point, I had read the first three books in the series, which I borrowed from the school library. She was going to be promoting the fourth book, which had just been published. I had decided that would be a good way to spend some of my allowance. I'd buy book four and get her autograph in the front! Well, that was the plan. But once I heard her speak, I decided I needed to own the whole set. She is the first author I have ever met, which makes the books even more special to me.

So, first up this summer is a re-read of this awesome series. This is the third time I have read them now. I love reading books I have already read. It's like visiting old friends. As I finish *Fenway and Hattie in the Wild,* I wonder if Victoria is working on anything new, so I decide to look her up online. I discover that she does this thing called *"Books in the Kitchen"* with another author, Elly Swartz, so I watch some of the episodes. They are really funny, and it looks as though Elly and Victoria are good friends, so I decide to see if our town library has any of Elly's books.

I go back online to the library catalog. Yes, they have all three of Elly's books. I run downstairs to ask Mom if she can take me to the library.

"I'm sorry, Sarah," she tells me, "but I promised Adam and Daniel I would take them to their baseball game this afternoon, and I just *have* to get some laundry done before lunch. But why don't you give your grandmother a call? I'm sure she would love to take you."

"Great idea. Thanks!" I head back upstairs to grab my phone.

"Gran, are you busy today? I need to go to the library, and Mom is too busy to take me."

"Sarah, honey, I'd love to take you. How about I pick you up in half an hour, and we can get some lunch before we go to get your books?" I grab my bag, change my shoes, and head back downstairs to tell Mom.

Lunch is delicious. We share a deep-dish pizza at Pizzeria Uno, then head off to the library. I find Elly's three books easily and decide to borrow all of them. I like the way she seems to write about kids who have some unusual problems. I check them out and go looking for my grandmother. I find her engrossed in the handcraft books. She has several of them in a pile on the floor and is flicking through one which seems to have quilting patterns in it. She looks up from the shelves when she sees me.

"Sarah, this was a great idea to come here! I'm going to borrow all of these and get some new crafting ideas." We head to the circulation desk so she can borrow her books. We both leave the library happy with our selections.

We are waiting at a red light on the way home when she turns to me and says, "Sarah, I've got an idea. Why don't we make this a weekly thing until you go back to school? I've really enjoyed our lunch and library time. What do you think?"

"Oh, yes please! I've had a really fun time, Gran. Thanks!"

"We'll check with your Mom when we get home, but I am sure she will agree."

When we arrive home, Mom, Adam, and Daniel have just gotten back from baseball. The boys are all excited because their team won. Mom is in the middle of putting out some juice and cookies for them and coffee for her. She adds another glass of juice and another cup of coffee, and the five of us sit outside and talk about the game, the library, and other events of the last few days. As she is about to leave, my grandmother tells Mom about her idea of us spending time together once a week. Mom says she thinks it is a great idea. I'm so excited. I can't wait till next week's lunch and library time.

Adam and Daniel spend a lot of time going to baseball practices and games, and I spend a lot of time reading over the next few weeks. I'm really enjoying my weekly trips to the library with my grandmother. Each week, we go somewhere different for lunch. Last week we went to this little place I had never heard of. It was quite a long drive away, so Gran picked me up earlier than usual. She told me that one of her friends had told her they make the best lobster rolls there, and she wanted to try one. We both had a lobster roll, and we shared some fries. What an amazing meal. I wonder where we will go tomorrow on lunch and library day.

I've got to wait a whole day for our library visit, and I've read everything on my bookshelf. I wander down to the living room to see if there's anything good on TV, even though I'm not a big TV fan. On the coffee table, I spot a book I haven't seen before. It's got a robot on the cover. But it doesn't look like any kind of serious book. The robot looks like it is blowing things out of its rear end onto a couple of kids. Doesn't look like my kind of book at all. I flick through the TV channels. Nothing interesting there. So I pick up the book and start to read.

EngiNerds by Jarrett Lerner grabs me from the first chapter. It's nothing at all like the kind of books I usually read, but it's different and it's funny. It must be Adam's summer reading book, I guess, since I know neither of my brothers would be reading a book unless they absolutely had to. I always think it's amazing that I can love something so much that they dislike so much. Anyway, I settle onto the couch and keep reading. By the time I hear Mom calling Adam and Daniel to come in and get ready for dinner, I have finished the book, and I'm developing quite a curiosity about the author.

After dinner I head upstairs, pull out my iPad, and look up Jarrett Lerner. I find out that he has a really interesting website, which has all kinds of activities that you can print out and work on. There are all kinds of fun things; there are writing, coloring, drawing, and lettering guides. I wonder if my brothers would like to do some of them. As I'm looking through, thinking about which ones I could print out for them, I come up with another idea.

"Mom," I say as I rush into the kitchen, where Mom is making herself a cup of coffee. "Can I please use the printer? I've got a surprise thing for the family that I want to print out."

"Of course, dear," she replies as she pours the cream into her coffee. "I think we are getting low on ink, but hopefully it will be okay for what you need to do."

I have my iPad with me, and I can print using our wi-fi, but the rule is that I have to ask first. Mom has never said no, probably because I have never printed very much. She has never asked what I'm printing, either, probably for the same reason. I send the print task, and as I open the door to Mom's study, I see that the printer has already finished its job. I gather up the papers and smile to myself as I think about my plan for using them.

SIX

COMING HOME FROM THE LIBRARY with Gran, with a copy of *Revenge of the EngiNerds,* as well as some books on robotics, I explain to her my plan. She laughs and says she can't wait to see the results. "It's pizza night tonight," I tell her. "So you won't have to wait for too long."

It's Daniel's turn to choose the pizza toppings, so, as usual, he chooses pepperoni and onion. I like onions, but I don't really like pepperoni much. No problem, though. It's easy to pick it off. I always give my pepperoni to Daniel, since he loves it so much. When I hear the doorbell ring, I know it is the pizza arriving, so I hurry downstairs with my pile of papers and box of markers. The rest of the family gives me some strange looks as they arrive at the table, but I don't say a word. I'm waiting till they all get here.

"I found this awesome book about farting robots on the coffee table yesterday," I announce. "Is it yours, Adam?"

"I guess so," Adam tells me. "I'm supposed to read it for summer reading, but I haven't started yet. Did you read it? Is it any good?"

"I really enjoyed it," I tell him. "Surprised myself, actually. I was desperate for something to read while I waited for my library day today, so I figured I would give it a try. It's funny and clever, but not anything like what I usually read. I'm glad you left it in the living room. You helped me learn a lesson about reading more of a variety. I even got the sequel from the library today. Thanks, Adam."

"Why do you have all this stuff with you?" Daniel asks. "Can't we just get on with eating our pizza?"

I explain that I looked up Jarrett Lerner and about all of the fun activities that I found on his website. I tell them that I think it would be cool to work on some of them together. Tonight's activity, I announce, is called "Gross Toppings for Pizza." Seems perfect for pizza night. Adam and Daniel actually seem quite excited, getting louder and louder as they share what they would put on their pizza.

"Shh!" I tell them. "Your toppings are a secret. Draw them on your paper while you eat your pizza, and we will all share at the end before we do the dishes." I distribute the papers, share the markers around the table, and start drawing my own pizza toppings.

"Gran is looking forward to seeing these," I announce when I see that Mom and Dad haven't started drawing yet. They pick up some markers, munching and drawing.

Once the meal is finished, the sharing and dishes done, as well as the voting on the grossest pizza (Dad won!), everyone agreed that we should do an activity like this every pizza night during the summer. I think next week's will be "Super Nasty Smoothie."

"That was a great idea, Sarah," Mom tells me as she puts the vase of flowers back into the middle of the dining table. "We definitely need to do more fun things together as a family, and that sure was fun. Who would have thought I would have had so much fun thinking of gross things while eating my dinner!"

SEVEN

EVERY YEAR, MY FAMILY RENTS a cottage on Cape Cod for a week. We always go there in August, usually the second or third week. It depends when Dad can get the week off of work. The wait always seems like forever to me, but it's finally arrived. Tomorrow we leave! The drive there always seems to take so long, much longer than the drive home. We always take Dad's car. It is bigger than Mom's, but that doesn't make it any more comfortable for the three of us who are squashed in the back seat. I hate sitting in the middle, but that's where I usually end up. We have too many things to take for a whole week away to make it possible to use the two seats in the far back. As usual we drive straight there not stopping at all, because we are all so eager to get to the cottage and have our week begin.

Finally, we arrive. There it is, looking exactly the same as it did when we left it a whole year ago. It's almost like time stands still. Adam, Daniel, and I get a little bigger each year, but the cottage remains the same.

I love this cottage. It is so different from our house. There are only two bedrooms, so, as usual, my brothers get one and Mom and Dad get the other. But that suits me just fine. I love sleeping on the daybed in the sunroom. I always look forward to the first night, when the bags are unpacked and the rest of the family has gone to bed and closed their doors.

After dinner, as I lie awake and imagine that I am here in this little cottage all by myself, I gaze across the living room at the string of seashells hanging from the ceiling, and the resin seagull that guards the cottage happenings from his perch in the rafters. For a whole week, this cottage is going to be my sanctuary, keeping me safe from a world I do not understand. Safe from all of the people I try so hard to be like. Safe from their judgment every time I fail. To be lying here tonight, on the very first night of the week, is exciting. It's Friday night, and we don't go home until next Sunday. There are lots of things I look forward to doing in Dennis, and I run through them all in my mind.

———

First on the agenda this year, as in other years, is a visit to an amazing store nearby, in South Yarmouth, called "Bass River Mercantile." We shop there at least once or twice every time we come to the Cape. It's the sort of store I can imagine Laura Ingalls Wilder shopping in. The building itself is two hundred years old, and as we step inside, we hear the usual squeaking floorboards. I thrust my fingers into the pocket of my shorts, searching for a quarter. When I find one, I place it carefully into the slot on the nickelodeon and pause while it rewards me by playing an old ragtime tune.

The best part of the store is that it feels just like you are entering another world when you walk through the door. It's almost like stepping through a wardrobe door and finding yourself in a magical land. There are so many different things to look at, admire, and perhaps buy, and every time you turn a corner, you find even more. I take my time and carefully examine each tiny treasure, each soft toy, and each seaside souvenir. Many of the souvenirs include real seashells, which I love to look at. In my mind, I store away ideas for things I can make myself at home. Today I also find a whole collection of mermaid garden ornaments. I'd love to buy one, but they are very expensive, so I decide to settle for picking up and admiring each one.

One thing I buy every year is the store's very own brand of soda. As I always do, I wait until I have thoroughly studied everything else before I make my way to the far back corner, where the shelves are lined with many different flavors, all in bottles with special labels that have a picture of the store on them. My favorite is orange, so I carefully put together a four-pack box and fill it with bottles of sweetness. Every year I say to myself that I will make them last, but every year they are gone by the end of our Dennis week. Maybe that is the way it should be. Something as special as this orange soda shouldn't have to risk being tainted by exposure to the real world. I wonder how long they will last this year.

As we leave the Mercantile, I notice that one of the seats outside the store has a life-size garden mermaid relaxing on it. I sit down next to her, admiring her and telling her how much I love mermaids. I guess I didn't notice the rest of the family heading back to the car. When Mom comes looking to see where I am, she just smiles, takes out her phone, and takes a picture.

Mom loves to shop, but it's not really a great favorite of mine, apart from the Mercantile, that is. As we are driving around sightseeing, we come across a store that we all agree needs to be investigated. It's called "Doctor Cavity's Candy Shop," and it is right next door to "Doctor Gravity's Kite Shop." The candy shop has handmade chocolates, so after examining each and every option, I choose a large slice of chocolate-covered caramel. That chocolaty deliciousness gets tucked away in my bag of beach supplies. When we get there, I will put it to good use! The whole family agrees that a visit to the Doctor will definitely be on our agenda next year!

Most of the time we are at the cottage, we eat our meals either at the dining table in the sunroom or at the beach, picnic style. At least once or twice each year, though, we visit "Kreme 'N Kone" which boasts "The Finest Fried Seafood Anywhere" on the sign outside the restaurant. I'm sure the fried seafood is very good, but my favorite, which I order every time we go, is broiled sea scallops with rice pilaf and coleslaw. Everyone in my family has their own favorites, so when we enter the restaurant after our visit to the Doctor, ordering takes no time at all. Delicious! And of course, as we are leaving, we get a soft-serve ice cream to go for dessert.

As much as I love Bass River Mercantile and Kreme 'N Kone and even spending time in the cottage itself, by far my absolute favorite part of our Dennis week is all of the time we spend at Mayflower Beach. It's only a few minutes' drive from the cottage, but the journey there always seems to take an eternity. The first visit of each year's week is always the best, I think.

Day one is always for sightseeing, shopping, and restaurant meals. But it's day two now, so we are off to the beach. Once we arrive in the parking lot, I know that I have hours of peace ahead of me. Hours where I can be me and not have to worry about what anyone else thinks. Hours where it doesn't matter if I can't sit still. I can just get up and go for a long walk, and no-one will question me. Hours where it doesn't matter if I can't concentrate on one thing for more than a few minutes. I can jump from one activity to the next without having to give an explanation to anyone. Hours where it doesn't matter if my thoughts are racing or if I think I am the ugliest person on the planet. I don't have to talk to anyone. I don't have to explain myself to anyone. I can lose myself here. Perhaps the person I find at the end of the day will be a better version of me.

Even though my dad is always saying how good salt water is for you, I have always hated the way it feels when it dries on my skin. I wouldn't make a very good mermaid, would I? Adam and Daniel spend most of the day in the water with their boogie boards, but I prefer to do a lot of different things. I set myself up with my beach towel, my books, and my plastic bags for collecting beach treasures. I set about examining the sand around me in minute detail, kind of like the way I examined everything in the Mercantile yesterday. I have a glass jar on my bookshelf at home. I have special places at home for my beach treasures. My sea-shells and my sea glass. My sea-shells and my mermaid tears.

When I was little, I used to take home bags and bags of shells, but now I am more selective. I fill my bags and bring all the shells back to my towel for closer examination. Only the very best will pass the test. As I study each one, I imagine their history. What kind of creature lived in the shell? Only occasionally do I find a piece of sea glass on this beach. Today I only find two small pieces. Those I will definitely keep, because they are so rare. I wonder what that piece of glass was before it found its way to Mayflower Beach. For all of these treasures, I wonder, how long have they been waiting on the beach for me to rescue them? And I wonder, when will someone rescue me?

After I have spent some time selecting beach treasures, I spend the rest of this first beach day reading. I love to lose myself in the world of the characters in a book. There's usually a problem the main character is facing. Sometimes the problem is a small one, one that is easily resolved. In other books, the problem is so big it is hard to imagine how they are ever going to solve it. But by the end of the book, they always do. They always figure out what the tough times are supposed to be teaching them and make plans to go on with their lives. I wish real life were that simple. I wish I knew how to solve my own problems as easily as many of the book characters solve theirs. I wish I could figure out what my tough times are supposed to be teaching me and make plans to go on with my life.

Most days I read at least one book. A lot of planning goes into packing for a vacation for me. A couple of years ago, my parents bought me an iPad, and for a while I downloaded books onto it. That sure made my suitcase a lot lighter! But I found that I really prefer to read real books. I love the feeling of turning the pages, and I don't have to worry about running out of power. So every day, I take the book to the beach that I am reading and the one I will read next. Usually that's enough. It is today!

At the end of the day, I pack everything into my bag. Books first, then my beach treasures carefully sorted into bags. The shells will be washed when we get back to the cottage and then added to the glass jar, which has a special place on my bookshelf when we go home at the end of the week. The sea glass will have an even more special place inside an empty orange soda bottle, which I keep on my bedside table. Sometimes when I can't sleep at home, I lie in bed and hold the bottle, remembering the special week at Dennis and looking forward to the next one.

All too soon, our wonderful week of the beach, reading, and freedom is over. Tomorrow we will be going home. The last night is always another sleepless one for me. Tonight, as I lie awake hour after hour, I have one extra thing to think about. Sixth grade. A new school. A whole new way of organizing the school day. All new staff to get used to.

Our last day at the Cape is always the same. We load up the car, clean the cottage, and set off for home. I don't think any of us are really in a hurry to leave, but Mom and Dad always have to push us to get the cleanup and pack-up done. Mom tells Adam and Daniel to sweep the floors, and although they complain, as they always do, they know that we never get to leave until the floors are cleaned to Mom's satisfaction, so they sweep as they mumble their complaints. My job is always to go around each room carefully, checking that we haven't left any of our belongings behind. I look under the beds, in every cupboard, and behind the couch. Nothing. Mom carries everything out to Dad, who loads the trunk of the car like a Tetris puzzle. There's always more to take home than there was when we came, and this year is no different. Mom just can't resist buying all kinds of things while we are here.

We always stop at the same place for breakfast on our way home. It's a restaurant that has been around since 1971.

Mom and Dad both used to visit with their families when they were younger, and it's fun to keep the tradition going. The restaurant is called "The Breakfast Room." Before we go in to eat, Mom takes our annual picture. She lines the three of us kids up in front of the sign with the two fried eggs for Os. She posts the picture on Facebook as we are going in to eat. It doesn't matter that people know we are away now, she says, because we'll be home soon. When we get home, I know she will add a copy of the photo to the wall in our living room. It's kind of cute to see the three of us growing, while the fried eggs stay the same.

I don't even bother to pick up the menu. I order the same thing I always order, pancakes and orange juice. My dad says they make the best corned beef hash around.

"You really should try this stuff," he says to us all as he passes around a forkful of corned beef, holding it in front of each of us. He tries this every year, but, as usual, we all pull a face and go back to our own meals. Even Mom says it looks "unappetizing" (that's the word she uses). Adam and Daniel aren't quite so polite. This year Daniel likens it to "dog barf," which causes Adam to start snorting his soda through his nose. Disgusting!

All too soon, our meal is over. Back in the car. Back to the real world. Our Dennis week is over for another year.

I look forward to our Dennis week all year.

It's like the only chance I get

to be myself.

But who am I?

How do you define a person?

Is it by what you can see?

Is it by their physical appearance?

Is that who I am?

If so, I am the ugly fat girl with blonde hair.

The girl who wears glasses and braces.

The girl who has too many pimples

to count.

Or is it by how a person behaves?

Then, I am the sometimes quiet,

but sometimes out-of-control girl.

The girl who likes to curl up for hours

with a book,

but who sometimes can't stay still for a single minute.

The girl who loves to help other people
and animals
but who cannot help herself.

Or is it by how others behave
toward you?
I am the girl others love
to bully.
The girl others don't choose
for sports teams
or project groups.

Or is it by what is inside a person?
I am the keep-my-thoughts-to-myself girl.
The don't-let-anyone-inside girl.
The people-will-only-hurt-you girl.

Dennis is my
"I don't have to worry about any of that"
time.
But Dennis is only one week.
One week

almost at the end of summer.

One week

closer to back-to-school.

One week.

I dread our Dennis week.

EIGHT

WHILE WE WERE IN DENNIS, Dad caught a few fish. He prefers to fish in lakes, but if there is water around, he will try fishing in it. Adam and Daniel spend a lot of time on fishing trips with him during the year, and I have to admit that I have always been a little envious of the amount of time they get to spend together. A while ago, I decided to try hard to show an interest too.

After our Dennis week, he decides that the family will go on a fishing trip to a lake near our house. Mom packs a picnic lunch, and all the way there, we discuss how many fish each of us will catch. To be honest, I don't really think I will catch any, but I announce that I will catch a big one. Adam and Daniel both laugh. Loudly.

No-one is successful before lunch, except Mom, who says her goal of relaxation was met. We eat egg salad sandwiches and drink cold lemonade and talk about whether we will have to stop and buy fish and chips for dinner on the way home. But not long after we put our lines back in the water after lunch, Dad gets a fish hooked. He is working hard to pull it in, but before he is able to get it out of the water, a huge eel slithers up and snatches the fish right off Dad's hook! My hook is still in the water, and a couple of minutes later, the eel, with Dad's fish still inside it, firmly hooks itself on my line.

After a moment of initial shock, Dad comes over and helps me land the eel-fish. Well, to be honest, Dad does most of the landing. I just hang onto the end of the rod. I am not at all keen on touching the eel. It is so slimy and slippery, but Mom insists that the family scrapbook needs a photo of this fascinating family event. So I hold the eel while she takes photos. Yes, *photos*. Not one, but dozens. Every possible angle, while I stand holding the disgusting creature. Finally, she puts her phone down, and Dad takes the eel from me. Together, we decide to put it back in the water.

"It has proved itself to be a better fisherman than me today," Dad announces. "It deserves to live another day."

We stop and buy fish and chips on the way home.

Dad is a very organized person. He says he has to be because of his job, but I think it is more than that. I think it is a part of who he is as a person. I think I get that from him. I love being organized. Being disorganized makes me panic and lose the ability to focus.

Dad pays close attention to even the smallest details. When he gets home from a successful fishing trip, there is a ritual he goes through before the fish are given to Mom to cook or wrapped to be added to the stash in the freezer. Mom hates this ritual and always makes sure she is in another room doing something very important, like vacuuming. But in an effort to spend more time with him, I have made myself into Dad's assistant.

The day after the eel-fish adventure, Dad arrives home from a day of fishing with some of his friends with a catch of two, so I set to work covering the kitchen counter with newspaper so that one by one, the fish can have their moment in the spotlight.

First comes the measurement. Dad has already measured them in the field to be sure they are the legal size to keep, but at home he wants an accurate measurement, down to an eighth of an inch. Once that is done and recorded in his notebook, the head comes off. My grandmother some-times cooks with fish heads, but that is something Mom refuses to do. So our fish heads always end up rotting in the compost heap, and Dad is sure that is why his tiny vegetable garden always produces such amazing crops.

Next comes a careful slice down the center, all the way down to the tail. The fish is opened up, and Dad does his medical examiner act on the corpse before him. Every little detail is examined and recorded. What are the stomach contents? How many eggs are present? All kinds of details. He has a separate section in his record book for each place he goes fishing so he can study patterns over time. He has notebooks going back to many years before I was born.

I am not at all interested in the insides of a fish. It's just all a part of me trying to make Dad happy by being interested in things he is interested in. I don't think he realizes how hard I am trying, though, because once the fish examination is done, he just walks away and leaves me to clean up. He doesn't say a word. I wish he would just say, "Thanks, Sarah. I appreciate your help."

Summer.

It's over.

Why does it always go by

so quickly?

School.

It hangs over me.

Like a giant storm cloud.

All summer long.

School.

I love learning.

I love routine.

I love organization.

So why can't I get my brain

to cooperate?

Why can't I focus for long enough

to make my teachers know

I am doing my best?

Why can't I seem to avoid

being labeled with words like:

Immature

Disruptive

Inconsistent effort

Doesn't work well with others.

Why can't I get anything other than

that dreaded letter

C

on my report card?

Why can't I get my parents to understand

that I really am trying my best

and that it is getting harder

and harder

to even keep earning that C?

I found out that I needed glasses last year.

I found out that others did not see life

as a blur.

I thought that would help.

I can see the leaves on the trees now.

But I still can't control my brain.

Teachers.

Every year they say things like,

"A new school year is like a new start.

Take advantage of it, Sarah!"

This year I'll be in a new building.

Done with Elementary School now.

On to Middle School.

Three years, then High School.

"These years are so important,"

they say.

Do they really think I don't know that?

Do they really think I don't try my absolute best?

"This really is a new start,"

they say.

I really wish I could believe them.

But how is it a new start when it's the same kids,

and the teachers will send progress records,

and warning notes about **that girl**.

NINE

MIDDLE SCHOOL. THE DAY HAS arrived. Michaels Middle School. Like all the schools in our town, Adams Elementary and Michaels Middle are named after men who were important in the early days of the town's history. Someday I think I will do some research on what Mr. Adams and Mr. Michaels did that made them so important, and why none of the schools are named after women. Surely there were some important women in our town's early years.

I'm so nervous as I walk through the main doors to the school. I really want to have a good three years in this building. My dream is to be able to make friends and do well academically. I'd like to be able to make that dream become a reality, but deep down I have serious doubts.

I remember from our orientation day how to find the classroom that will be my home-room this year. My home-room teacher is Mr. Douglas. It's quite obvious as soon as you step into his classroom what he is interested in. Sports. There are baseball curtains and football curtains, and baseball posters and football posters. Like I said, sports! He seems okay, though. He smiles a lot and likes to tell jokes. He has the craziest laugh. He says that our sixth-grade year is going to be the best year ever! I'd really like to believe him.

There's a new student in our home-room who moved to this town over the summer. His name is Giuseppe. I don't know where he has moved from, but when Mr. Douglas asks us all to share something about ourselves with the class, Giuseppe shares that his family only moved into their house two weeks ago and that they are still unpacking boxes. That must be really hard, to pack up your whole life into boxes and start again someplace else. My family has lived in our house since I was two years old. I'm not sure I could cope with moving. The real me, that is. The mermaid me would swim away without hesitation.

Mr. Douglas is also going to be our ELA and social studies teacher. That explains the huge classroom library on one whole side of his room. I can't wait to dive into that and see what he has that I have not already read. We get to move to different rooms for all of the other subjects, not just for specials like at Adams Elementary. I think it is really going to help me to be able to move between periods and have different teachers. The classes mix up a bit, too, so I won't always be with the same kids. Maybe this is going to be a new start after all.

Day one. It's going pretty well. We have home-room, where we all receive our schedules for the first term of the year. Home-room time will usually be a much shorter time, but for the first day, there are always lots of questions (especially from us sixth graders) about schedules and how things work, so they give us extra time. I take a look at my schedule, and it seems quite straightforward, so I ask Mr. Douglas if I can look at the class library.

"I have the largest classroom library in the school, and I buy new titles every month," he tells the class. He sounds as though he is proud of that, so I am guessing he likes to read too. He explains that we are always welcome to borrow anything from there and that he works on the honor system. No signing out. No due dates. No borrowing limits. Just make sure to bring them back when you are done so others can borrow them. And it would be nice if we could put them back in the right places, but he isn't going to hold his breath. I have to say, I am pretty excited to find myself staring at a whole wall lined with books, just begging for me to read them. I choose two titles, sit down, and start reading.

For the rest of the morning, we move around, getting to know who our teachers will be for art (I hope she is not like Mr. Miller) science (How many more times do we have to learn about the scientific method? It's not like the process is likely to change!) and math. Then it is time for lunch.

We have a routine in my family. After dinner and before the dishes are done, my mother brings out onto the dining table all of the things my brothers and I can choose from to make our own sandwich for our school lunch for the next day. We usually get to buy our lunch at school on our birthdays, but last night, Mom told us we could buy it today as a treat for the first day back. I think the real reason might be that she has not been grocery shopping since we got home from Dennis, and the fridge is looking pretty empty. Anyway, whatever the reason, I am pretty excited about this change in routine.

Lunch-time arrives, and the whole sixth grade starts moving toward the cafeteria. I am a little overwhelmed by the size of the cafeteria. I don't remember if we saw it during orientation, although I'm pretty sure I would have remembered it if we had seen it. Michaels Middle is a lot larger than Adams Elementary. There are two elementary schools in our town, but just one middle school, so half of the students I haven't met before, not just the new-to-town kids like Giuseppe. I guess that's all part of the new-start thing too.

I thought lunchtime was noisy and overwhelming last year. But I am just not prepared for what is about to happen. At least half of the grade has arrived before me. I join the line, waiting to buy my lunch. Soon my tray is piled high with nachos, chocolate milk, and sliced oranges. I love nachos. Delicious odors fill my nostrils. No assigned seats, so I head for the back of the room, where I can see there are some empty tables.

I don't see it coming. Maybe because I am concentrating on carrying my tray instead of studying my feet, which is what I usually do when I am walking. Maybe it just happens so suddenly that I wouldn't have noticed even if I was looking down. I'm walking along with my tray. Then my tray and I are both on the floor. Nachos everywhere. Before I even have time to comprehend what is happening, the custodian is beside me with a mop.

"Could you be more careful next time?" he sighs as he begins to clean up my mess.

I look up and one of the lunch ladies is coming towards me. She tells me she saw what happened. A boy at one of the front tables stuck his foot out as I was walking by. No wonder I went down! Sometimes I can be pretty clumsy, not at all like a graceful mermaid, but I have never fallen while walking in the cafeteria before. I feel both relieved and horrified. She doesn't tell me which boy it was, and it is probably better that way. She tells me I can come and get some more lunch, but I say no, that's okay, I'm not really that hungry. I ask to be excused to go to the bathroom to remove the remnants of the nachos. I make sure I don't get back until it is time for lunch to be over.

"How was lunch?" Mom asks when we arrive home that afternoon.

"Delicious!" I yell as enthusiastically as I can. I head up-stairs to my room to do my homework. I don't really have any homework, since it's just the first day of school, but the last thing I want to do is have any further conversation about lunch. I drop my school-bag onto my bedroom floor and grab my soda bottle of mermaid tears as I throw myself on my bed. One day done. One hundred and seventy-nine to go. How on earth am I going to survive?

The next few days pass relatively uneventfully. As I get off the school bus, I start to think about the weekend, but I also reflect back over the week. We have met all of our teachers and started receiving homework from most of them. I'm actually pleasantly surprised about the home-work. I was expecting to find a big increase in the amount from last year, but so far, it's not been too bad. My favor-ite this week has been ELA. Mr. Douglas said that he just wants us to read for half an hour each night in preparation for our first book project in a couple of weeks. Reading. I can handle that!

For once, I spend a whole weekend doing almost no reading. That first week of school was exhausting, and I feel as though I just need to do nothing. I play a few games on my iPad and hang out in the yard, watching the clouds. That's something I've enjoyed doing since I was quite small. I can remember lying on the back lawn, staring up and searching for animals in the sky. Sky art, Mom called it. "Did you have fun doing sky art today?" she would ask me when I came inside. I wonder why I am enjoying doing something that I used to do when I was so small. Perhaps I am reluctant to grow up.

Now that it's the second week of school, we are back to our usual routine at home. Mom is a kindergarten teacher at a private school in another town and doesn't usually start back to school until at least a week after we do. She always jokes that it's her favorite week of the year. Dad's at work, the kids are at school, and she gets to enjoy lots of alone time. She always says it in a joking kind of way, but I am sure there is a fair bit of truth to it. I don't blame her!

Once Mom is back at work, we are back to the routine of my grandmother coming over after school for an hour or two until Mom gets home. Gran is a little weird, but like, in a really good way. She likes a lot of things that you don't normally think of as being grandmother things. I think she has seen every episode of *Dr. Who* enough times that she could recite the scripts. She drives a blue MINI Cooper, which she calls Tardis. It even has *Dr. Who* stickers all over it. She joined a group of MINI owners a while ago, and sometimes they go on rallies. My grandmother has been on several. One time she invited me to join her. It was amazing. There were forty-five MINIs all driving in a line through the towns and the countryside. We even had a police escort, so all other traffic had to stop and let us go by first. I loved seeing the faces of the people we passed; many of them were counting and looking as if they just couldn't believe what they were seeing.

I get off the bus and see Tardis parked in our driveway. My brothers and I speculate on what will be waiting for us for a snack as we walk into the house. (It is brownies. With crunchy edges, just the way I like them.) Adam and Daniel don't have any homework, so they start watching some of their favorite after-school television shows. I head upstairs to start working on my science worksheet and to do my reading. No math today. Yay!

I'm just getting started when there is a soft little knock on my door. I know it's not either of my brothers. They don't knock. They just barge in and make demands. I open the door to find my grandmother holding a plastic bag full of yarn. During the summer, she taught me to crochet, and I had been talking with her about wanting to crochet a mermaid, but I did not expect to see what she was holding.

"I love the idea of you wanting to use your new crochet skills to make a mermaid," she says. "I thought I would get you some supplies, and we can work on it together each day when you have finished your homework."

I look in the bag. There is a pattern, some flesh-colored yarn for the body, purple for the tail (she knows purple is my favorite color), and a really beautiful shimmery purple for the hair. I am so excited. I throw my arms around my grandmother's neck and thank her. I can't wait to get started. I complete my science sheet as quickly as I can, promise her I will do my reading in bed before I go to sleep (she knows I like to do that anyway), and we get started on my mermaid. It is much more difficult following a pattern than just doing random stitches, but by the time Mom comes home and my grandmother leaves, I have finished the top of her head. I should say *we* have finished the top of her head, because it really has been a joint effort so far. We set the goal of getting up to the eyes tomorrow, homework permitting.

Mom says she is too tired to cook after her first day back. She says kindergarten kids have far too much energy!

So when Dad gets home from work, we order a pizza. We don't even go out to pick it up, as we usually do if we are ordering pizza. We have it delivered. Pizza with some more of my grandmother's delicious brownies for dessert. This was an extra pizza night for the family, so I don't have a fun sheet printed out. We just eat and listen to Mom describing her day.

Later, when I go to bed, I feel as though it has been a pretty good day. Giuseppe came over to sit with me at lunch, so I wasn't sitting by myself for the first time this year; my grandmother helped me get started on my next mermaid project; and we had my favorite pizza for dinner (it was my turn to choose, so it was chicken and broccoli). I wish Patricia wouldn't turn and walk in the opposite direction every time she saw me in the hallway, but I am glad she is not in any of my classes, because that would make things really awkward.

I feel quite content as I settle into bed to read.

TEN

ACADEMICS HAVE ALWAYS BEEN A challenge for me. Apart from reading. When I was really little, Dad used to read me a book about a donkey as a bedtime story. I loved that book and wanted the same story every night. I'm pretty sure Dad must have gotten tired of reading the same story, but I never got tired of hearing it. It was about a donkey who had some problems with his friends and his life, so he ran away from home. Eventually he realized that things were much better at home than out in the world on his own, so he went home, where he was welcomed by his friends, who had missed him. When I look back on it now, I wonder if that story was maybe making a prediction about my own life. I think that donkey and I have a lot in common.

Eventually, Dad had read that book to me so many times that I knew it by heart, so as well as having it as my nightly bedtime story, I would often sit on my bedroom floor and read it to my bears and dolls. Then one day, according to my mother, she found me sitting on the floor reading them a different story. At first she thought I must have learned that one as well. But when she saw me a few days later reading another one, she realized that I was actually reading, not reciting. I am sure there were some wrong words in amongst it all, but the essential point was that I was reading. No-one is really sure how it happened.

When I started school, my teachers were impressed by my skills, as well as a little concerned. While they were teaching basic phonics skills to the rest of the class, what were they going to do with Sarah? I didn't really have too many problems in the early years at school, but once we started receiving grades for our work, things slowly started to change. Sometimes we would receive a grade for work we did in class, but more often it was for a project we had to complete at home or for a test we had to study for. I really did try my absolute best, but my best just never seemed to be good enough.

I love to be creative. I love to draw. To write stories. To create clothes for my dolls out of scraps of yarn and fabric. Yet somehow, when I had to create a project, even when it was one about a book I had read and enjoyed, I had great difficulty. My Mom always said she would buy any materials I needed, but I had to show her a plan first. That seemed fair. For some reason, no matter how far in advance of the due date I began planning what I would do, it always seemed to be a last-minute rush to get it done and ready to hand in.

There would be lots of yelling from Mom and Dad and demands that I learn to plan my time more wisely. Reminders that they knew I was quite capable as they waved their arms around, indicating the evidence of my creativity on show in my bedroom. There would be lots of tears from me and screaming that I was trying and had worked on it every day. Then there would be the inevitable C. It just didn't seem to matter how much I was enjoying the book or the topic, the end result was always the same.

Studying for a test was even worse. Our teachers would tell us in advance what material would be on the test. The information we needed to learn was in our notebooks or our textbooks. But that was exactly where it would remain. In my notebook or my textbook. It did not seem to be able to make the leap into my brain. Another C.

This is the academic history I bring with me to middle school. A reputation as a student who doesn't really care enough about her work to put in her best effort. A student who hands in last-minute, rushed work. A student who obviously does not use the study guides teachers have shared to prepare for tests. A student who has little regard for the importance of following through and producing appropriate grade-level work. All things I have seen over and over on report cards.

I have tried so hard to figure out why this was the case. Why did I have so much difficulty with academics, but my own personal projects were no problem? Was it that schoolwork always came with deadlines, while my reading and knitting and drawing and writing were just for my own pleasure and could be finished anytime? If I could read and enjoy a novel, why could I not read a textbook and master the information it contained? If I could write a story about the imaginary adventures of my dolls or mermaids, why could I not complete a written report for school without a great deal of difficulty?

Was I putting too much pressure on myself? Was I not putting enough? I had always believed I was doing my best, but perhaps I really wasn't. I have tried many times to talk to Mom and Dad about it. They ask me about how school is going, about my grades, about tests I am studying for. They have even asked my teachers, who then ask me. It's all a huge circle of confusion. I've tried to explain the difficulties I am having, but I just can't seem to make them understand. I guess I shouldn't really be surprised by that, since I can't even make myself understand. They keep telling me I am just making excuses. Perhaps they are right. Why can't I just be like everyone else? Why can't I just be normal?

My cafeteria strategy over the next few weeks is to get there as quickly as I can and head immediately to the back, looking for an empty table. I don't really understand why the front tables always fill up first. If you sit there you have to eat your lunch with other kids constantly pushing by you. There are always empty tables at the back, until the stragglers finally make it into the room. And for some reason, Giuseppe now chooses to come and sit at whatever table I have chosen.

As we eat our lunch, there's not a lot of conversation at first, but eventually I figure out the reason he started coming to sit with me. "I noticed how you always borrow lots of books from the class library," he tells me. When he doesn't add anything more, I say, "Yes. I like to read, and Mr. Douglas has got a lot of books I haven't read before. And I like how he trusts us just to borrow them and then put them back. Much easier than the school library." Giuseppe eats several more mouthfuls of his sandwich before he says anything else.

"I like to read too," he says. "At my last school, the other guys couldn't understand why I wanted to read more than I wanted to play video games or sports. It caused me a lot of trouble sometimes." Interesting. Someone else who has had difficulties with their classmates.

I've had problems with classmates for quite a while now. Sometimes it seems to me that whatever I say, wear, or do is wrong in the eyes of my classmates. It's never-ending. Their eyes watch me, waiting for me to do something. I feel those eyes following me throughout the day. I hear the whispering and the giggling. If I drop a book, it's hilarious to everyone around me. The eye rolls whenever I would give an incorrect answer in class convinced me a long time ago not to raise my hand. But worse than all that are the loud comments, right to my face, about all the ways I am a waste of space.

I'm curious. "How did you handle that?" I ask. Giuseppe looks thoughtful for a minute before he answers. "In the end, I learned to pretend to like what they liked and to read where no-one could see me," he says quietly.

So after that, we discuss books as we eat lunch. He likes to read Rick Riordan and other fantasy series writers like him, whereas I prefer realistic fiction, although I do read a variety of fiction, as well as any books I can find about the mythology of mermaids. Although there are not a lot of actual books we have in common, it soon becomes clear that we both share a reading passion. Before long, I actually start to look forward to lunch time as a highlight of my school day.

Eventually, Giuseppe starts to share more of himself during our lunch time talks. I find out that his family moved to our town during the summer because they lost their home in a flood. They used to live in Florida, and in a really bad storm, they lost everything they owned except for the few things they were able to grab quickly and load into their car as they evacuated their town. Apparently when they went back after the storm and found their home beyond repair, his parents decided they did not want to rebuild. They wanted to move far away. They stayed in a hotel for a while so the kids could all finish their school year and they could figure out what they were going to do next. They decided to come to Massachusetts because they have some relatives nearby.

I am overwhelmed by this story. What an absolutely horrible experience to live through, yet he always seems to be smiling and happy. That's a lot to think about. I decide right then that I have to get to know Giuseppe better. Maybe I can learn from him. His family has faced something much more dramatic than anything my family has ever had to face, and he has obviously learned a lot about how to deal with difficult classmates. The mermaid me feels very relieved that he swam into my part of the ocean.

"I'm glad you came here," I tell him. And I mean it.

ELEVEN

IT DOESN'T TAKE LONG, THOUGH, before the workload of middle school starts to overwhelm me. Each teacher's expectations and demands seem to grow daily, and my ability to keep up seems to shrink just as rapidly. I begin to feel more and more overwhelmed and less and less able to cope. It becomes even more important to me to secure my masks in place. But underneath those masks, even though I don't want to admit it to myself, things are getting really out of control.

I feel as though I am running on an empty battery. The things that used to recharge me no longer have any effect. Reading. Writing. Drawing. Creating. They hold no attraction for me now. Even my once-treasured crocheted mermaid lies discarded in the bottom of my closet, the eyes on her armless, tailless body staring out at me accusingly.

I'm dragging myself through each day, my feet heavy. Like rocks. Like mountains. Now, more than ever, I wish I really could just turn into a mermaid and swim away. The water currents would carry me along, and the weight in my feet would be gone. But all there is in my life is mermaid tears. Lots and lots of mermaid tears, which I have to work hard to hide from the world.

My body and my brain are in slow motion. Teachers are saying my concentration is even worse than usual. Mr. Douglas is the only one who asks me if there is anything he can do to help.

"You seem to be having difficulties lately, Sarah. How can I help you?" He sounds concerned. I like Mr. Douglas. Which gives me more guilt. I should not be worrying him or taking up his time. And then comes the day.

The day when I do not have a finished social studies project to hand in to him. The day when I have to say, "I haven't started it yet," when he asks me where my two-week project is. The day when Mr. Douglas tells me he is disappointed and that he will need to email my parents to let them know that he will give me a short extension, but the project has to be done. The day when I am afraid to go home, because I know what will happen once my parents get home from work.

———

Grounded. That means different things to different people. To my brothers it means not being allowed to ride around after school or on the weekends on their bikes or to watch television. They have to work on something quietly inside. Actually, that's usually a punishment for the whole family, because Adam and Daniel are the worst at doing anything quietly. For me, being grounded means that I am not allowed to do any of the things I love. Reading. Writing. Drawing. Creating. The things that used to re-energize me. The things I now have no desire to do. I can't believe my parents have not noticed this. I must be too good at securing my masks firmly in place, even at home.

Every afternoon until my social studies project is finished, I have to sit at the kitchen table with my grandmother so she can be sure I am actually working on it. My grandmother is witness to my shame. I don't know how she can bring herself to speak to me. I am such a failure. I have let her down. She has always trusted me to be doing my homework upstairs in my room while she supervises my brothers downstairs. Now she knows I am not to be trusted.

"Gran, I really am sorry about this," I tell her when the project is finally finished. "I didn't do this on purpose."

"I know that, sweetheart. Believe me, I know. I'm sure the work is getting harder as the year goes on. I just want you to know that you can always ask me for help. Okay? I'm not just here to make snacks and keep Adam and Daniel quiet, you know. I'm here for whatever you need."

I truly don't know how to respond. Asking for help is really hard. Even from my grandmother. I know it is something I need to work on.

The social studies project is just the beginning. The further we get into sixth grade and the more the workload increases, the more difficulty I seem to have. I have never believed myself to be unintelligent, but now I begin to wonder if that is actually my problem. I look around at my classmates, and they seem to be coping with the curriculum without too many problems. Perhaps I have earned all those C grades because that really is my ability level. I know I have worked hard, and I have always really thought I would one day earn better grades to reflect my effort. But that one day never seems to come, and maybe I now know why.

———

I think it would be safe to say that math is my biggest problem. Always has been. Mr. Johns, the sixth grade math teacher, makes no secret of the fact that he does not think I am mathematically inclined. Every year I would wish that the teachers would begin with geometry. I understand geometry. I even enjoy it, well, kind of. But geometry always comes quite late in the year, almost as if it's a topic to keep for when our brains are beginning to switch off toward the end of the school year.

This year, we begin with a whole unit on fractions. My worst nightmare! Actually, I don't think I am alone in feeling that way, judging by the facial expressions of my classmates! We convert improper fractions to mixed numbers. We convert mixed numbers to improper fractions. We multiply fractions. We divide fractions. And just when I think we are all ready to scream, "Enough!" Mr. Johns tells us we are moving on to decimals, which are only slightly better. I try really hard to be patient while I wait for geometry.

Last year in science, I enjoyed learning about the solar system. With my grandmother's obsession with anything to do with space, and *Dr. Who* in particular, we had lots to talk about in the afternoons once homework was finished. We made up all kinds of stories about the adventures we would have if we were exploring the solar system and beyond. We imagined that her MINI Cooper, Tardis, really was a Tardis. Able to travel through time and space. After my grandmother would leave to go home, I would go upstairs and write the stories, often including my dolls and bears in the adventures we had on distant planets.

This year, science doesn't seem to have quite the same appeal. We studied the scientific method in fourth and fifth grade, so it seems rather repetitive to be studying it again. We talk, this year, about how important it is when studying anything in science to keep an open mind. Mr. Powell, our science teacher, tells us that by sixth grade he often finds that students have formed some ideas about things they think are true or not true, and we have to make sure we are open to changing our minds in the face of evidence we discover during our investigations. That sounds pretty reasonable to me. It makes me think that we will be making some exciting discoveries this year. But then he shares the topics we will be studying this year. Matter. Motion. Energy. Nothing very exciting there!

Some of the engineering topics do sound quite interesting, though. Mr. Powell tells us that later in the year we will have the opportunity to choose a common engineered system, such as a refrigerator or a cell phone, and evaluate its impact on the daily life of humans. He says he thinks we might like to start thinking now about what we will choose to study, and he reminds us about being open to evidence. Even though we love something, like a cell phone, we will need real evidence, not just our opinion to show that it has changed human life for the better. Everyone giggles a little at that, which I am sure he is expecting. We all have cell phones, after all, and I am sure we all believe we cannot possibly live without them!

In fourth grade, we learned to play the recorder as a part of our music lessons at Adams. We learned to read music, play tunes, and we even got to compose music of our own. That was fun. I enjoyed practicing my own compositions, but after a while my family was unanimous in their demand that I practice at the far end of the garden, under the apple tree. I can't say that I minded that too much, though. The apple tree never complained about me making too much noise or playing the same tune over and over again.

By fifth grade, we had to choose an instrument to play in the school band or orchestra. I started learning the clarinet, but I have to admit I was not very good at it. It took me quite a while to master the art of just getting the thing to make a sound at all. Blowing through the reed on the mouthpiece was not at all easy.

I had really hoped we might be able to stick with music theory in sixth grade, but no such luck. After a long talk with my parents, I decided to switch from orchestra to chorus. It wasn't that I thought that I had a great singing voice or anything. In fact, I really don't enjoy singing at all, but I thought I might have a better chance at being a little more successful in chorus than I had been playing an instrument. It was a real shame that playing the recorder wasn't an option! As the weeks go by, our folder of music is bulging with new songs we are working on. Some of them are actually quite fun to sing, but there are just so many of them. Of course, we have to learn the words in preparation for our concerts. At least with orchestra we had the music to follow. At this point I am seriously beginning to question my decision to drop the clarinet.

I think the hardest thing for me about being at Michaels Middle, though, isn't the workload or the music or anything that actually happens in the building. The hardest thing is what doesn't happen. The fact is, I miss Patricia's friendship so much. She has continued to avoid me whenever she can. I hoped that time would soften her feelings toward me, but no such luck. It's so hard to sit on the same bus as her to and from school every day, never being able to speak to her. I've tried telling her how sorry I am, but she walks by me as if she hasn't heard. She always sits behind me on the bus, and I can feel her eyes boring a hole in my back. That hole is getting so big now that sometimes I feel as though everything that is inside me is going to fall out.

I'm grateful to Giuseppe. I really enjoy sitting with him at lunch, and I do feel as though we are becoming friends, not just people who eat lunch together. But I'm also a bit uncomfortable about this friendship. I've never had a friend who is a boy before, and I don't want anyone thinking I'm trying to get him to be my boyfriend. And I don't want people to start picking on him because he hangs out with me. I like him too much to want that to happen.

I'm confused. I'm nervous. I'm scared. Middle school is hard.

TWELVE

MOST OF OUR TEACHERS ARE responsible for just one subject, except Mrs. Paul and Mr. Douglas. Mrs. Paul is our teacher for physical education and health, and of course, Mr. Douglas is our ELA and social studies teacher. Health is not bad. We actually get to work on some pretty interesting group projects. My favorite one was earlier in the year when we looked at the influence of different forms of media on our health choices. My group studied the influence of television and concluded it had a pretty strong influence!

Physical education is something quite different, however. I hate it. I am not good at it. I never have been any good at anything physical, and it seems to me that as I work my way through puberty, my overweight body does not become any more suited to the sorts of activities that Mrs. Paul demands of it. At the beginning of the year, Mrs. Paul shared with us that one of the goals of the year was to enjoy our physical activities. Honestly, I cannot see that ever happening, but I do try my best.

Sometimes we have group challenges, where we have to choose from the equipment Mrs. Paul puts at the front of the gymnasium to do things like transport the whole group from one side of the room to the other. There are always rules of one kind or another, such as only one team member can be touching the floor at a time. The idea is that we have to work together, communicating and coop- erating with the other members of our team, or we will not be able to complete the challenge.

I don't mind these activities so much, because they put the whole class on a much more equal footing. Those who are really good at sports are not necessarily the same ones who are good at these challenges. Brainpower is important too. If only one person is allowed to touch the floor, we can often find ways to get everyone except the last team member to the other side, so we have to refine, or even completely change, our plans and designs. I feel pretty good about being able to contribute some good ideas to the groups I am working with and even better when it is one of my ideas that they decide to go with. I might have a struggle with fitness circuit goals, but using my imagina- tion is something I am good at.

Today our goal is to get our group to the other side of the gym in the shortest amount of time. This is a new facet to the challenges. We have half of the period to plan and prepare, and then Mrs. Paul will time each group. The pressure is on. We all go up and study the available equipment, then come back to our group corner and start planning. We try out several plans before we settle on one that we think will work. There are five groups. Mrs. Paul draws numbers, and my group will be timed last.

We sit nervously watching as the other groups all take their turns. Mrs. Paul records their times on the rolling white board. The other group times are all fairly close together, and we feel sure we can do better. Our turn comes at last. We get up, get our equipment together, and get ready to start.

"Go!" Mrs. Paul shouts as she pushes down on her stopwatch.

We are off. Our plan is to move the whole group at once, so there will be no need to add extra time by going back and forth, as the other groups have done. We are confident. All I have to do, along with two other members of my group, is to sit on a mat that other group members will pull with jump ropes we've tied to the corners. That seemed easy when we practiced. We sat close together in the middle and wrapped our arms around each other while clutching the edges of the mat. But I don't think any of us were prepared for how bumpy the ride would be when we were on our timed run.

Just when we think we are certain to win, I lose my balance. I can feel it happening, but I can't do anything to stop it. I lean over to my left, knocking Shannon into Kevin. Suddenly, all three of us are on the gym floor, our dreams of victory dashed.

We weren't competing for a trophy or a cash prize or even a homework pass. But you would have thought it was the end of the world if you were observing the reaction of my teammates. I don't enjoy being competitive, although I do like to master a challenge. My teammates yell that it is all my fault and beg Mrs. Paul for another chance. Unfortunately, there is only enough time left to pack up the equipment and get ready to go to the next class, she tells us.

She compliments all of the groups on their very different design ideas and tells us that in our next class we will begin training for the cross-country run. Perhaps it is the thought of cross-country training, as much as our team's rather dramatic failure, that causes Shannon to be so angry, and perhaps I should just take a deep breath and straighten my mask. But when she screams at me, "It's all your fault, Sarah. We would have won if it weren't for having to drag a fat lump like you along!" I just snap.

Shannon is one of my frequent tormentors. She seems to really enjoy saying nasty things to me. It seems like she picks on me for practically everything I do. What I am wearing. What I say, especially when we are working together in a group project. Actually, it feels like even the way I breathe is wrong, as far as Shannon is concerned. And because she is so popular, she is always really good at getting others to join in the taunting. Suddenly, I can't take any more. I grab the nearest thing, my water bottle, and throw it at her. She screams as it hits her shoulder, losing its lid and emptying its contents all over her shirt. Of course, Mrs. Paul hears the scream, and despite my protests that Shannon started the confrontation, I am sent to the principal's office.

Mr. Harris has no sympathy when I try to explain the incident to him either. Before I know it, he is leaving a voicemail message for my parents. Assaulting another student is unacceptable behavior, he explains, with a mandatory in-school suspension, which I will serve in the office tomorrow. If they have any questions, they should call him. They will have questions. I am sure of that. But they won't be for Mr. Harris. They will be questions for me, and I won't be able to answer them.

I remember when I was reading about Atargatis, that her baby daughter, Semiramis, had grown up in the royal household. Eventually she became Queen Semiramis, and as well as leading military campaigns (which was really unusual for a woman at that time), she is believed to have been responsible for many building projects. Apparently, many historians believe that one of these projects was the famous Hanging Gardens of Babylon, one of the seven wonders of the ancient world.

I had heard of the Hanging Gardens, but I didn't know very much about them, so out came my iPad. I found out that they were a series of tiered gardens containing a variety of trees, shrubs, and vines. The foundation for the garden was made of mud and bricks. Apparently, the gardens are the only one of the seven wonders whose exact location has never been confirmed by archaeologists. There are some researchers who believe that evidence might exist beneath the Euphrates River, but they can't excavate there. Other researchers think the gardens never really existed. They think they were just the subject of ancient artistic imagination.

It makes me wonder. Were Atargatis and Semiramis really women in ancient history, or are their stories just legend, not fact? Did the Hanging Gardens ever really exist, or did an artist just dream them up one day, and their idea got copied over and over as the years passed? Who is to say, and who will know many thousands of years from now, when the stories of our own lives are told, which parts are historical fact and which parts are just legend? And will it really matter in the end?

I'm becoming desperate to become a mermaid and swim away. To have the ocean hide my tracks. Hide my very existence from history.

Another explosion.

Violent.

Explosion.

Shattering.

Destructive.

Blowing apart.

I have tried so hard

to keep the combustion inside.

But it's not working.

Not today.

Inside my brain

everything is out of control.

Calm one minute.

Destroying everything around me the next.

The shock waves

radiating outwards.

No end

to their destructive power.

Why is it so hard
to be like other people?
Why is it so hard
to be normal?
Perhaps it would be better
if I wasn't even here.

THIRTEEN

GROUNDED. AGAIN. MORE LECTURES. BUT worse than that, I think, is hearing my parents' raised voices well into the night when I suppose they think my brothers and I are asleep. Blaming each other. Accusing each other of not being firm enough with me. Questioning what they have done wrong. Arguing about what they should do to make me understand, once and for all, that I need to learn to behave and focus on things that matter before it is too late. I just lie in my bed and listen to it all. Powerless. So tired of feeling powerless.

The next day is, without a doubt, my worst ever at school. I have to spend the whole day in the school office, with teachers delivering my work for each period. Everyone who comes to the office during the day sees me sitting here and knows why I am doing my work here for the day. And there are many visitors to the office throughout the day. Parents. Teachers. Other students. Lots of other students. I can feel their eyes on me. I can feel their judgment on me. I feel my judgment on myself. My life feels as though it is completely out of control.

This in-school suspension will go on my permanent school record. There is absolutely nothing I can do to make this incident go away. It doesn't matter to anyone why I exploded. What matters is that I lashed out physically at a classmate, and, as Mr. Harris made quite clear, if I were to behave like this when I am older, I would probably find myself in trouble with the police. Yes, I'll admit, that scares me.

Sitting in the office, I realize something very important. My coping strategies, which have not been particularly successful of late, are now no longer working at all. My masks are no longer in place. What is inside me is making its way to the surface. I am no longer capable of pretending that the actions and words of others are not hurting me.

I have been picked on, ignored, and straight-out bullied for a long time now. I have tried very hard to not let on that the pain inside of me is immense. Pain built upon pain. I have tried very hard to not let on that the pain hurts. Deeply.

There is pain in the fact that no-one seems to be interested in hearing my side of any of these incidents. Not the teachers. Not my parents. They want explanations, but not excuses, they say, but I can't give explanations that will satisfy them. If I try to tell them about what others are doing to me, I get the "Just ignore them" or the "Move away and do something else" type of responses. I don't understand what is happening to me, and I don't know how to explain what it is that is happening inside of me.

There is pain in the fact that all of the things that used to calm me no longer have that effect. Spending time with my books, my art, my writing, my dolls, my soft toys. They all used to calm me. I have been made to feel that dolls and soft toys are for little kids, and I should have grown out of them by now. I have no creative thoughts inside of me to write or draw. Pain built upon pain.

The ride home on the school bus is awful. I certainly expected some judgmental looks, and perhaps even some comments from my fellow passengers, but the reality is worse than I could possibly have imagined. I take my seat and do my very best to keep looking forward, to block out what I can see and hear. The journey home seems to take an incredibly long time today. Pain built upon pain.

My grandmother meets the bus, standing by the mailbox until the doors have closed behind me. She doesn't ask me how the day was. But she does tell me she has made brownies for an after-school snack for the three of us, and that she will be happy to help me with any homework I have. Such a small gesture, but it means a great deal to me.

"Crunchy edges on those brownies?" I ask her.

"Of course, sweetheart. I always make them the way my Sarah likes them." I hug her silently before going inside to begin the after-school routine.

My concentration was not the best at school today, and all of the work my teachers assigned needs to be completed and handed in tomorrow, so there is quite a lot of homework. My grandmother sits with me patiently as we slowly work our way through one subject after another. My mother arrives home long before I am finished, but my grandmother insists on staying until I am finished. "She had a lot of homework today, and she's been working really hard on it," she tells my mother. "I'd love to stay and help. I think we are on a roll with this today."

We finally finish just before my father arrives home from work. Mom insists that my grandmother stay for dinner, and I am relieved when she agrees. I notice that the talk at dinner is about everything except school, which is fine by me. My brothers have lots to tell about their sports activities, which are coming up over the weekend, and I am happy to allow them to monopolize the conversation.

After dinner, I hug my grandmother and thank her for the brownies and the help. I think she knows that she has helped me in ways that I cannot even begin to put into words.

My grandmother and I have always had many things in common. We both like to read and talk about what we are reading, and we both like to make things. She taught me how to knit several years ago, and since then, my dolls have received lots of handmade sweaters and scarves. I love it when she takes out some of the beautiful embroidery work that she has done over the years and tells me the story about how it was made. About three years ago, she moved to the town where we live. Before that she lived about a two-hour drive away, so we did not get to see her as often.

I remember when we used to visit her at her old house. She would prepare for our visit by placing a treat for each of us on her kitchen counter. We'd go in, say hi, and claim our treats. I'm the oldest, so my treat was first in the lineup. Then my brother Daniel's treats. Then Adam's treat. It was always the same treat, but we knew which one was for each of us. When we had eaten our treats, my brothers would head out into her yard to play.

My grandmother had a really big yard at that house, much bigger than any other I have seen. I always thought it was big enough for four houses. She had an enormous vegetable garden down at the far end, where she would grow all of the vegetables she ate throughout the year. During the summer she was always busy gathering her crop and filling her freezer. Then during the rest of the year, she got to enjoy the fruits of her labors and her garden. I remember thinking it was amazing to think of never having to buy vegetables at the store. She also grew strawberries, and when they were in season, we were allowed to go and pick some to eat straight from the garden. Those ones were the best!

Sometimes I would go outside too, but I really preferred to play inside, with her little ceramic duck family, which sat on the edge of her kitchen counter. A mother, a father, and a baby duck. I would create all kinds of complex storylines for them. When I got home from each visit, I would write and draw their adventures. Sometimes they would meet with mermaids in my stories, and they would all swim around, exploring the oceans together. I loved those ducks. So cute, but so fragile.

My parents would warn me over and over again to be careful with them, which I always was. But one day the inevitable happened. The baby duck slipped out of my hand and lost his head on the hard kitchen floor. I remember it vividly. My sorrow for the duck. My fear of the punishment that I was sure would follow. But my grandmother simply went over to a drawer, took out a tube of glue, and all was well again. I thought she was so understanding. I knew she really loved those ducks. They had been a gift to her from a special friend, and she had treasured them for many years. But that day I came to realize that she loved me more. I thought my grandmother was so clever that she could fix anything. She fixed my fearful, sorrowful heart. I knew the baby duck would survive. I knew my grandmother was not angry.

I wish now, with all my heart, that my grandmother could open a drawer, take out a tube of glue, and stick together all of the cracked and broken pieces of my brain and my life.

Who am I?

How do you define a person?

Is it by what you can see?

Is it by their physical appearance?

Is that who I am?

If so, I am the ugly fat girl with blonde hair.

The girl who wears glasses and braces.

The girl who has too many pimples

to count.

Or is it by how a person behaves?

Then, I am the sometimes quiet

but sometimes out of control girl.

The girl who likes to curl up for hours

with a book,

but who sometimes can't stay still for a single minute.

The girl who loves to help other people

and animals

but who cannot help herself.

The girl who sometimes
could sleep for days
but sometimes stays up all night.
Drawing.
Reading.
Walking.
Talking to her dolls.
Sleep not needed.
Or desired.
Too much energy.
Mustn't stop.

Or is it by how others behave
toward you?
Then, I am the girl others love
to bully.
The girl others don't choose
for sports teams
or group projects.

Or is it by what is inside a person?
I am the angry girl.
The out-of-control girl.

The selfish,

Inflict-my-rage-on-others girl.

That's what they say

is inside me.

I am the keep-my-thoughts-to-myself girl.

The don't-let-anyone-inside girl.

The people-will-only-hurt-you girl.

I have a secret.

A huge secret.

One I can't share with

anyone.

If anyone were to find out,

it would ruin everything.

I am working very hard

to keep my secret.

I have decided I cannot do this anymore.

I cannot live this life.

I am going to become that mermaid

I have always imagined myself to be.

I am going to find a new part of the ocean.

I am going to swim away.

I am going to disappear.

My exact location will never be known.

Like a mermaid,

the ocean will hide me.
One day people will wonder,
Did she ever really exist?

I don't know yet
where I will swim to.
Perhaps to Dennis.
I always feel much better there.
Or is that too obvious?
Perhaps I should swim
much farther away.
Perhaps, like a mermaid,
I should make the whole ocean
my playground.

I've always imagined mermaids
to be happy and content with their lives.
I may not have their beauty,
but I will have their freedom.
Freedom from everything
and everyone
that has held me back.

I want their life.

Quiet contentment.

Mermaid tears

washed away.

No need for masks.

I will keep my secret

until it is time to swim away.

PART TWO

"The sea, once it casts its spell, holds one in its net of wonder forever."

- Jacques Cousteau

FOURTEEN

MARCH IS MY BIRTHDAY MONTH. I'm a Pisces, like At-argatis. There's an old nursery rhyme that's supposed to predict what sort of person you will be based on the day of the week you were born. I was born on a Friday, and my mother used to recite the rhyme to me when I was little, telling me it meant I was going to spend my life being a really good person. (She also told me that gay meant something different back in the 1800s, when it was written.) She also used the rhyme to help me learn the days of the week, although it was quite a while before I could actually recite the days without adding all the parts about the children!

Monday's child is fair of face
Tuesday's child is full of grace
Wednesday's child is full of woe
Thursday's child has far to go
Friday's child is loving and giving
Saturday's child works hard for his living

And the child that is born on the Sabbath day
Is bonny and blithe, and good and gay.

I didn't question the words for Friday when I was younger, but I certainly do now. I try to be a good person, I really do. I try to be loving and giving to my family and everyone around me, but over the last year, maybe more, that person seems to have been replaced by someone even I do not like.

At first the changes were gradual. I won't say I didn't notice them. I think it was the building pattern I didn't notice until it was too late. Until I lost all my friends. Until I got to the place where I am now. So far behind in my schoolwork that it seems impossible to ever catch up. Until my grandmother will not allow me to go upstairs after school until she has seen all of my completed homework. Until I can see the disappointment in her eyes that I don't want to work on the crocheted mermaid with her. Until my parents are constantly grounding me, even though there is nothing left that I care enough about to miss while I am being punished. Until I no longer care about any of the things that once brought me joy. Reading. Writing. Drawing. Creating. Until there are no drawings decorating my room. Until my jar of shells is gone. Smashed to pieces. Discarded with the trash. The only thing I have saved from myself is my soda bottle of mermaid tears. But it is no longer on my bedside table. I simply do not trust myself. It is tucked away, deep in my closet. Behind my spare blankets. Out of sight. Not yet safe because not yet out of mind.

Yesterday was the first day of March. It will be my birthday in six days. On your birthday, people usually say things like, "Wishing you a wonderful year ahead!" I don't think I can endure another year like the last one. Or has it actually been longer than that since my life spiraled out of control? Since I lost even the vague concept of who I am that I had been clinging to.

My birthday falls on a Friday again this year. I'm going to try to convince my parents that I'm not feeling well so I won't have to go to school.

One of the things Mr. Douglas does for his homeroom kids' birthdays is to have a birthday lunch. You get to choose a few friends to join you in the classroom, where you can eat, chat, listen to music, and generally enjoy not being in the noisy cafeteria. Everyone seems to really like it. Some kids just bring their own lunch from home or go down to the cafeteria and buy something before they come back to the classroom, but Mr. Douglas doesn't mind if you want to organize something like a pizza party. Several kids have had pizza delivered for their birthday lunch. I think it's a really nice thing for him to do, giving up his quiet time like that. But I am in a panic about it. I don't know who I would invite to join me. I'd ask Giuseppe, but I'm still uncomfortable with the whole boy-girl thing. A year ago, my choice would have been easy. It would have been me and Patricia for lunch. I've come to the point of accepting that we will never be friends again, but it still hurts. As much as I dislike being in the cafeteria, I would actually rather just eat my lunch there like it was any other day.

As the school week goes on, Mr. Douglas mentions it several times. There are actually two other birthdays in our class this week, which makes me think about it and stress about it even more. I haven't told Mom and Dad about this class tradition, because I am still planning on saying I am sick. I don't want them to be suspicious.

"I'm looking forward to having lunch with you tomorrow, Sarah," Mr. Douglas says to me on Thursday as we file out at the end of the day.

"Me too," I mumble as I leave the room, avoiding eye contact with everyone. Especially Mr. Douglas.

The next morning, I try. I try really hard to convince my parents I am not feeling at all well and will need to stay home from school. They both say they cannot possibly take the day off work, which is what I had expected them to say. Usually when one of us is sick, my grandmother comes over for the day. She fusses over us so much that you end up feeling kind of smothered with kindness.

I start to think about what it will be like to be home with her on my birthday. I am sure she will think that it is terrible to be sick on this day of all days and will fuss over me. That would just make me feel too guilty. I can't be that dishonest to my grandmother! So I tell Mom I am feeling a little better and that I think I can manage to go to school.

As I sit on the bus, I agonize over what I am going to do. By the time I arrive at school, I still have no idea how I am going to deal with the problem. All morning, I go from class to class so completely distracted that I am not even sure what subjects I go to, let alone what work is assigned.

Then lunch-time comes, and I head for homeroom. Mr. Douglas meets me at the door. I still have no real plan. I will just say that I'd prefer to eat in the cafeteria and hope he will accept that. I open my mouth to tell him that, but what comes out shocks even me.

———

"Mr. Douglas, can we just have you and me for lunch, please? I have a big problem, and I need to ask you if you can help me."

What? Where did that come from? When did I decide to share myself with Mr. Douglas? In the split second before Mr. Douglas gets his facial expression under control, I can tell he is rather surprised too. He looks thoughtful for a moment before he responds.

"Sarah, I am so happy you feel you can trust me. I have a suggestion though. I promise to make the time to talk with you before the end of the day, but why don't we make lunch-time just about celebrating your birthday? Why don't you grab some friends and come back to eat?"

I can't help myself. I certainly don't mean to do it. I scream at him, "Don't you understand? I don't have any friends! Everyone hates me! There's nothing to celebrate! I wish I had never been born!"

Just then, Giuseppe walks up to the classroom door, where this exchange has taken place. I know he must have heard it all, but he doesn't show any reaction. He just says, "Hi, Sarah. I remembered it was your birthday today, and I wondered if maybe I could join your birthday lunch."

We have spent most lunch-times over the last couple of months as the only two occupants of the far back table in the cafeteria, and although we've been slowly getting to know each other more over that time, and I really am beginning to think of him as a friend, I am still uncomfortable about the thought of my classmates taunting me about my "boyfriend." I feel a twinge of guilt, knowing he heard me say I have no friends. He's been good to me. What I said just wasn't fair.

"Great idea, both of you," Mr. Douglas answers for me. We follow him into the classroom.

For a birthday lunch, the twenty minutes are more subdued than celebratory, but we manage to make conversation and eat our sandwiches. I barely taste my lunch or register what either of them is saying. I am too focused on questioning what I have done, asking Mr. Douglas for help. I definitely didn't plan to do that. Deep down, I do recognize that I need help. I do know that I cannot continue the way I have been for the past year or so. I do acknowledge to myself that Mr. Douglas is a person I feel I can trust; but, seriously, what can I expect him to do?

When it is time to go, Mr. Douglas tells me that we will talk after the math period, when he will be able to step out of the classroom because the reading specialist is coming in to do a lesson. I'm so nervous during the math period that I have no idea what we learn!

Once everyone is settled and Mrs. Colton is ready to begin her lesson, Mr. Douglas whispers to me that we can head down to the library. We will be able to find a quiet corner there, he says, and we can talk about anything I want to share with him.

When we get to the library, we find that there are only a few students there working with a teacher. We sit in the comfortable chairs on the other side, and Mr. Douglas reminds me that I can tell him anything that is troubling me, and he will do his very best to help.

I don't know where to start. He sits waiting patiently while I struggle to find words. Eventually I start talking. I tell him everything. Once I start to talk, I can't stop. Everything pours out of me.

I tell him about how I am having such difficulty with school-work. I tell him how I seem to have sabotaged all of my friendships, and that those who I used to consider to be friends are now those who are the ones who are bullying me the most.

I tell him how my parents just cannot understand my behavior, and the pressures it is putting on my family. I tell him about no longer feeling any joy from the things I used to love. I tell him how sometimes I feel so absolutely exhausted I can barely drag myself through the days, but sometimes I feel as though my body and brain have so much energy flowing through them that I can do absolutely anything.

I tell him that I truly believe the world would be a better place if I were not in it, and that I have decided to leave. I tell him I don't know where I am going to go, but I know my family will be better off without me there to mess things up for them.

He listens silently, nodding encouragement for me to continue. Finally, when I have no more left to share, Mr. Douglas looks at me.

"Sarah," he says quietly, "you do realize that this is something I can't keep to myself, don't you? I want you to come with me to speak with Mrs. Shelby."

I nod, and we both get up and head for the guidance office. I follow behind him, my mind racing, wondering what will happen next. A part of me feels a huge sense of relief. I have shared all of my secrets at last. All of these things that I have tried so hard to keep sealed up behind the masks are now out in the open.

I have told Mr. Douglas everything, and he has accepted every word without judgment. He told me before we had lunch that he would help me, and I am beginning to believe him. Perhaps it is going to be possible for something to change. As we continue toward Mrs. Shelby's office, I try to tell myself to trust that it really can happen.

FIFTEEN

MRS. SHELBY'S OFFICE DOOR IS open, so we know she is not speaking to another student. Mr. Douglas knocks softly and asks her if we can both come in and share something with her.

"Of course! Come on in, Sarah. It's good to see you. What can I do to help the two of you?"

Mr. Douglas and I sit down at her conference table, while Mrs. Shelby pulls up the rolling chair that she had been sitting on at her computer station. Mr. Douglas is watching me. I guess he is waiting for me to start telling Mrs. Shelby all of the things I just shared with him. But somehow my brain just will not connect with my mouth. I feel completely drained of energy. Of the ability to do anything more than sit there, waiting for whatever will happen next.

Finally, Mr. Douglas asks, "Sarah, would you like me to tell Mrs. Shelby the things you told me in the library?" I nod. "If I say anything that doesn't sound right, just say so, okay?" he adds. I nod.

And so, it begins. I sit and listen to my innermost thoughts and feelings being talked about, and I feel powerless to even move. I notice that Mrs. Shelby is taking a lot of notes as she listens, and that she keeps looking across at me. Perhaps to see if I have anything to add. Perhaps to see if I am going to react to hearing my life discussed like this.

Mr. Douglas starts talking about my grades and the fact that lately I have been receiving "Incomplete" several times, and even two D grades. Mrs. Shelby slides her chair back over to her computer and pulls up my academic record. She studies it quietly for a few minutes before turning back to me.

"Sarah, is there anything else you want me to know?" she asks. I shake my head. They both wait, I guess to see if I will change my mind and decide to share something else. Finally, Mr. Douglas speaks.

"I think the thing that concerns me the most is that Sarah has shared with me that she is planning to run away. She seems to be really serious about this plan, because she tells me she thinks that her family, and even the world, would be better off if she were not here."

Mrs. Shelby looks across at me. I nod. Finally, she speaks.

"I want to thank you both for coming and trusting me with this very important information. Sarah, I want you to go back to your classroom with Mr. Douglas and collect your backpack and anything else important that you need. While you are doing that, I am going to call your parents and ask them to come here, so that we can all sit down and talk about what needs to happen next. When you have everything, Mr. Douglas will come back with you, and we will take it from there. Does that sound okay?"

I feel confused. My parents will both be at work. Mrs. Shelby must be picking up on my confusion, because she adds, "Don't worry, Sarah. They will both understand me contacting them at work. Sometimes there are things that happen that are so important that we need to speak to both parents, rather than the person who is your emergency contact. I know that is your grandmother, but believe me, your parents will be very glad that I am going to call them. Don't worry. I promise this is the right thing to do."

Mr. Douglas guides me out of the office, and we walk back to the classroom in silence. The reading lesson is coming to a close, and I notice Mr. Douglas go over and whisper something to Mrs. Colton. She nods and tells the class, "Good news! No social studies today. We get to read a little longer!" Everyone sounds pretty pleased about that. Independent reading is a favorite with many of my classmates, and no social studies means no social studies homework.

I collect my backpack and jacket, and I am about to open my desk to get my homework out when Mr. Douglas whispers to me, "Don't worry about that tonight,Sarah. Consider it a little birthday present. I'll make sure to clear it with all of your teachers."

We head back to the guidance office, where the three of us await the arrival of my parents. I wonder what Mrs. Shelby said on the phone. What has she told them is so important that they should both leave work and come to the school as soon as possible?

The next few hours pass in something of a blur. My parents arrive at school within a few minutes of each other, and before long we are all seated around Mrs. Shelby's conference table. Mr. Harris is there too. Mr. Douglas and Mrs. Shelby talk about all the things I had told them. I watch Mom and Dad. They keep looking at each other, and at me.

"How could I not have known things were this serious?" my mother asks. My father just shakes his head and says nothing. Finally, my mother turns to Mrs. Shelby and asks, "What do you think we should do next?"

"I would strongly recommend that you take Sarah to the Emergency Room to be evaluated. I'll give you a copy of all of the notes I've made this afternoon, and the doctors there will know what questions to ask both you and Sarah. How do you feel about that?"

My parents look at each other and nod. My mother calls my grandmother and warns her that she may have to stay longer with my brothers and that she will call again when she knows what is happening. I can tell my grandmother is asking a lot of questions, but my mother just keeps saying that she will call again when she has some news. Would my grandmother please make something for the boys for dinner if necessary? Thanks. Yes, anything you all feel like. Of course, get a pizza if that is what they want. Tell them we will celebrate Sarah's birthday another day. Yes, let them have ice cream too.

I ride with Mom, and we follow Dad in his car to the hospital. We ride in silence. Mom keeps her eyes firmly fixed on the road, and I can see how she is feeling by the way her white knuckles are gripping the steering wheel. While Dad and I sit in the waiting area, Mom goes to the desk and has a rather lengthy conversation with several people. I notice her hand over the folder Mrs. Shelby gave her. Soon after she comes to sit with us, a nurse comes out and sits down with us too.

"Someone will see you soon," the nurse tells me. "Meanwhile, I'm just going to hang out with you while you wait. Do any of you need anything?" My parents shake their heads. I'm not sure what I do.

I wonder how this birthday has gotten so off track from the day we had all planned.

PART THREE

*"It takes generosity to discover the whole through others.
If you realize you are only a violin, you can open yourself
up to the world by playing your role in the concert."*

- Jacques Cousteau

SIXTEEN

QUESTIONS. SO MANY QUESTIONS. PEOPLE coming in and out of the cubicle in the Emergency Department of the hospital. Doctors. Nurses. Social workers. Others whose titles I don't know. Questions. Blood pressure. Questions. Blood draw. Questions. Physical examination. Questions.

My parents sit quietly at the side of the room, answering questions that are put to them and listening when questions are put to me. Questions about me. Questions about family health history. Does anyone in either Mom's or Dad's families have a history of mental health disorders? Are any of us hungry? They can get us something to eat. No, we are not hungry, thanks. We just want to know what is happening.

Finally, a doctor who has been in and out of the room a number of times comes back and sits down in front of my parents. I can see my mother take a deep breath as the doctor begins to speak.

"My colleagues and I believe the best possible course of action would be to admit Sarah to our psychiatric ward for a full assessment. We're concerned about what we have learned about how she has been feeling and behaving, and she has told her teacher and us that she believes her family would be better off if she were not here. We would like to do a more detailed assessment over the next couple of days and make a decision based on what we find about where to go from here."

I can hear my mother softly crying. My father takes her hand before nodding to the doctor.

"We agree. What do we need to do? Is there paperwork to sign? Does one of us need to stay with her?" Dad asks.

"We can do the paperwork shortly," the doctor responds, "and you can accompany her up to her room and help her get settled, but we do ask that you leave after that so we can begin to get to work figuring out what is happening. One of the nurses will come back in a couple of minutes, and we will get all of this underway. Do either of you have any other questions for now?"

Both of my parents shake their heads, and the doctor disappears around the privacy curtain. For the first time since we arrived, Mom, Dad, and I are alone in the room.

"I'm sorry," I mumble.

"Sweetheart, you have nothing to be sorry about," my mother replies. "We are the ones who should be saying sorry. We had no idea there was something wrong. I guess we have both been so busy with our own stuff, we haven't taken the time to notice the pain you were in. We promise we will do anything we need to do to help you. Anything at all. We promise."

Just then, one of the nurses comes from behind the curtain with a pile of papers for my parents to sign. Another person comes in with a computer on a cart, recording answers to yet more questions. After a few minutes, the doctor comes back, along with a man with a wheelchair.

"Ready to take a little ride, Sarah?" he asks me. I sit in the chair with a blanket tucked around me as we head for the Emergency Room elevator. The nurse and my parents come with me on the journey to the ward where I will be spending the next couple of days.

As we get out of the elevator, we are met by a nurse who greets us cheerfully. "Hi, Sarah," she says to me as we begin moving down the hallway. "I'm glad to meet you. I'm Brenda. I'm going to show you where your room is and help you and your parents get you settled. If there's anything you need, just let me know. I am sure you are all probably hungry. I know you were downstairs for a long time. I'll try and find you something to eat once we are all settled."

We enter a small room. There is a bed, a bedside table, and a tray table. On the wall is a small television. I can see that there is a small bathroom off to one side, while on the other side are windows that look across at another of the hospital's buildings. The lights are on in all of the windows, even though I know it is late. I wonder if the hospital ever sleeps, or is it like me when I am having my high-energy times. Sleep impossible, and not needed.

Once I have changed into a hospital gown and my mother has tucked me into bed, Brenda asks again if we would like something to eat.

"We will eat when we get home," my mother says, "but I would like Sarah to have something. She hasn't eaten since lunchtime at school." Even though I say I am not hungry, my mother insists, and Brenda goes off to see what she can find.

She comes back a few minutes later with some cereal, milk, fruit, and ice cream. "Sorry for the odd combination," she says. "The kitchen is closed at this hour, but this will keep you going, and I promise we will get you a nice healthy breakfast in the morning." To keep my mother happy, well, as happy as she can be under the circumstances, I eat it all and thank the nurse. My mother says she will be back in the morning with some clean clothes for me, before they both kiss me goodbye and leave.

As I lie in bed, I think about all of the times I had imagined in the Dennis cottage that I had the whole place to myself. Imagination and reality are such different things. Suddenly, with no family around, I feel so incredibly alone. After a few minutes, Brenda comes back and sits down in the chair in my room.

"I'm going to sit with you for a while," she says. "In a few hours, when my shift ends, another nurse will come in and sit with you. Her name is Jean. If there's anything you need, you just tell one of us. Now, I have something here that will just help you to relax and hopefully get a good night's sleep."

Brenda hands me two little plastic cups. One has some water, and the other contains a small white pill. I tip the pill into my mouth, swallow the water, and settle back into the bed. With the amount of noise that I can hear from the comings and goings in the hallway outside my room and with the strangeness of my surroundings and the outcome of my birthday, I do not expect to get much sleep. I am wrong.

I wake up the next morning to see a nurse, who I presume is Jean, leaning over me and whispering, "Good morning, Sarah. Let's get some breakfast organized for you." At home we often have scrambled eggs for breakfast on Saturdays, but as I pick at the eggs, which appear in my room a short while later, there is nothing about the experience that makes me feel as though I am in any kind of familiar surroundings. By the time I have finished eating, my mother has arrived with a bag of clothes and a concerned expression.

"Hi, sweetheart. Did you manage to get some sleep?" I nod. "I've brought you some clothes, and your grandmother has sent your birthday present. I'm sorry it's opened, but the nurses had to check what I was bringing in."

Mom hands me a half-wrapped package. I can see blue ears sticking out of one end of the wrapping. My grandmother knows my love for bears, so I expect to find a blue bear inside.

Instead, there is a bear mermaid. Yes, a really cute bear with a mermaid tail, complete with a little skirt and T-shirt. My mother is saying something about my grandmother being concerned that I would feel I was too old for the gift, but I am not really listening. I am too busy hugging my new friend.

After I have dressed and cleaned my teeth, another nurse comes into the room and tells us that one of the doctors will be coming to talk with me very soon. My mother can stay until then, but it will be best if I talk to the doctor by myself. My parents can visit again this afternoon, she tells us. They will take very good care of me until then, she assures my mother.

The doctor who comes into my room a few minutes later introduces himself to my mother and to me and explains that he and I will be going to his office for a chat. A chat sounds so relaxed, like something you would do with a friend. The knots in my stomach tell me this will not be like anything I would ever do with a friend. I hug my new bear as I follow Dr. Ogden out of the room, down the hallway, and into his office.

I am surprised by the appearance of his office. I don't know what I was expecting, but it wasn't this. The furniture is brightly colored, and when I sit down, I discover the chairs are as comfortable as they look. Lots of paintings cover the walls, and there are a number of healthy-looking potted plants on the desk, the top of the filing cabinet, and the floor.

Dr. Ogden sits down in one of the chairs beside me, not behind his desk. He asks me about my bear, so I tell him that yesterday was my birthday. He wants me to explain to him why I am in the hospital, so I recall the events of the most unusual of birthdays. He asks me questions. I answer them the best I can. I am surprised to discover that as we talk, the knots in my stomach begin to untie themselves.

I know that we must have been talking for a long time, because after a while there is a soft knock on his office door. A nurse apologizes for interrupting us, but she needs to know what I would like to have for lunch. Really? Lunchtime?

After she leaves, Dr. Ogden tells me that we will take a break for a while, but we will talk again this afternoon when my parents get here. He says that he wants to talk to them, and then we will all talk together. My bear and I go back to my room, where Jean and my lunch are both waiting to greet me.

While I wait for my parents to arrive, I eat and figure out how to work the television remote. I always name my bears and dolls, so while I eat, I study my mermaid bear and think about what I will call her. Eventually, I decide on Shelley, since she has a lovely iridescent scallop shell on her T-shirt.

SEVENTEEN

MY PARENTS SPEND A LONG time in Dr. Ogden's office. I try to distract myself with the television, and Jean makes a really good attempt at engaging me in conversation, but I think the majority of my brain is focused on speculating about what is being said behind that closed door. Finally, another nurse comes in and says they are ready for me to join the meeting. Shelley and I follow her down the hallway.

The first thing I notice when I walk in the room is that my mother has been crying, and my father is holding her hand. "Come on in, Sarah," Dr. Ogden says cheerfully. I sit in the same bright yellow chair as before.

"Sarah, I am so glad you are here," Dr. Ogden begins. "I know we can help you overcome the difficulties you have been having. You made a really good decision to trust your teacher and share with him what has been happening in your life." My mother squeezes my hand and tells me again that she is sorry she did not figure out for herself that things are much more complicated than she and my father had thought.

"I think the important thing we all need to focus on is that we can change things going forward," Dr. Ogden tells her, "rather than worrying about what we think should have been done in the past. Sarah, I've talked with your parents, as you know, and I feel as though I have a good understanding of what has been happening. Unfortunately, it is the weekend, and a lot of the people who will be working with you won't be back until Monday, but we can start right now to help you work all these things out. I'm going to be the head of your team, and your parents and I have the start of a plan worked out for you." I glance across at Mom and Dad, who are both looking at me and trying to seem relaxed.

Dr. Ogden continues, "Sarah, you are going to be staying here for a little while. Maybe a week or two. We will reevaluate your stay as we see how things are going. I am going to set up a number of things for you to do while you are here. You will get to talk to a therapist, do some school-work, meet with some other kids in small groups, and you'll be talking with me a lot. We're also going to try you on some medications, which I am sure are going to help you to feel more like yourself again."

He pauses for a moment, looking at me. "How does that all sound to you?" he asks.

What do you say when a doctor tells you that you have to stay in the hospital, and you didn't even know you were sick? I nod, looking across at my parents.

"You think this is the right thing to do?" I ask them.

"Yes, we do," my dad answers. "We know that you need help, Sarah. Actually, we all do. Dr. Ogden said that we are going to get some family counseling as well to help us understand all of this and to learn how we can all work together better. Your mother and I know that we both have a lot of work to do. But we agree with the doctor that this is how we need to get started. Don't worry; we are not just leaving you here. One of us will visit every day, and Dr. Ogden has assured us that there will be lots of great people taking care of you here."

He pauses and looks across at my mother, who I can see is trying to appear cheerful. She nods and takes my hand again.

"Sarah, things are going to get better," she says. "We all have to work hard together to make that happen. I believe Dr. Ogden when he says life is going to be a lot easier for you going forward. Will you trust us all to help you?"

"Yes," I whisper. I feel so completely overwhelmed. All of this attention on me, but not one word of reprimand.

Not one word telling me I am not good enough. Not one word telling me I need to control myself. Not one word telling me that I should not take my anger or frustrations out on other people. Not one word of judgment. Not one word of negativity from anyone else in the room. Just the flood of horrible judgment swirling around in my brain, from myself.

How on earth am I going to turn all of that off and focus on the future? Is Dr. Ogden really right? Are things going to be different? I had convinced myself that I was ruining my family, but Dad has said the whole family needs help, like it is a family problem, not just a me problem.

This idea will take a lot of getting used to!

Why is it so hard

to be like other people?

Why is it so hard

to be normal?

I had thought it would be better

if I wasn't here anymore.

Perhaps these doctors and nurses

really can help me to be normal.

I am trying to have hope.

Hope

that there is a normal person

inside of me.

Hope

that she can find her way out.

Hope

that the next year

will be different from the last.

Hope.

EIGHTEEN

IT IS SURPRISING HOW QUICKLY a new situation can start to seem quite ordinary. I have only been in the hospital a few days, but already the routine of life on the ward seems as though it is something that I am very familiar with.

After breakfast each morning, I have a few hours of school-work. The work isn't too challenging, but the teacher has explained that attending the hospital school for the morning will count as attendance at my school. I guess that is important. After lunch, I meet with Dr. Ogden for a while. He always starts our meetings by asking me questions about how things were before I came to the hospital, and I always try my very best to answer him as honestly as I can. It feels very strange to be talking about these things after trying so hard to keep it all hidden behind my masks for so long.

Later each afternoon, I meet with my therapist. The first day I met her, she told me to just call her Ellen. I liked her as soon as I met her. She has a way of making me feel comfortable talking to her. Perhaps it is her smile. Ellen smiles with her whole face, even her eyes.

We talk a lot about relationships. About how difficult and complicated relationships can be for everyone, and how we all need to develop skills to be able to get along well with other people. We talk about how sometimes we can hurt our friends' feelings, but that doesn't mean we can never be friends with them again. Sometimes family relationships can be put under a lot of strain, too, Ellen tells me, and for all sorts of reasons, but there are always ways to repair these relationships if we truly want them to be better. She tells me that we will work together with my parents on making our family as strong as it can possibly be.

I tell Ellen how I really feel as though I am a failure in every aspect of my life. I have not been able to keep friends, I explain, because I have not treated my friends well. I tell her about Patricia, and Shannon, and all the many incidents and people in between. She asks me the same question my parents and teachers have often asked me. Why? Why had I reacted that way? Why had I behaved in a way that later I would tell myself was wrong?

I still do not know the answer, but Ellen tells me that she will help me figure it all out. There is a reason, she assures me, and once we discover the reason, we can begin to work out solutions.

"You're making it all sound so easy," I tell her. She smiles and says, "Well, Sarah, unfortunately it won't be easy, but we will work on it together, and I promise we will come up with some solutions. There is nothing you have told me that is not solvable." She takes my hand. "I promise we can make things a lot better. I hope you can believe me."

Both Ellen and Dr. Ogden have made the same promise to me. They have told me that what has been happening is not my fault, but I'll admit I am finding this hard to understand. If it isn't my fault, whose fault is it? And why am I still in the hospital, nearly a week later? I'm not sick, am I?

This is really all so confusing, but everyone keeps telling me that I will understand soon, and everything will seem much brighter. I try very hard to believe all of this positive talk.

Saturday marks the end of a week in the hospital. My parents both arrive early in the morning to visit and to meet with both Ellen and Dr. Ogden to talk about what will happen next. We all sit down in Dr. Ogden's office, and I notice how much calmer my mother seems than the last time we were all here together. He closes the door and addresses us all.

"Good morning, everyone. It's such a beautiful day today; I thought it might be nice to go outside for a while once we have had a chance to talk about a few things. How does that sound, Sarah?"

I clutch Shelley to me. I haven't been outside in a week. It sounds like a great idea, but I am strangely nervous. The ward has been a sheltered world that has kept me safe for a whole week. A week of no conflicts. A week of feeling at peace with myself. A week of not having to worry about letting my family or myself down. A week of not having to worry about the other kids at school. What is wrong with me? It isn't as if I want to stay here forever. Do I?

"That would be nice," I answer finally.

My mother has visited me every day since that weird birthday last Friday, and every day she has told me how sorry she and my father are that they allowed this to happen by not realizing much sooner that something was wrong. She tells me how they blame themselves for being so busy with work and with getting my brothers to all their sports games and everything else in their hectic lives. She tells me that none of this is my fault, but hearing her feeling guilty just makes my own feelings of guilt stronger. Dr. Ogden has a lot to say about that as soon as we are all settled in his office.

"Sarah, your parents and I have already spoken about this, but I want to explain it to you now. From talking to you this week, and from reading everything your teachers have sent me during the week, I believe that you have a mental health condition known as bipolar disorder. Believe it or not, you are actually quite lucky. Many people don't get diagnosed until they are well into their twenties, and by then their lives are often completely out of control. You are young, and I am very confident that we can get this all managed very well, and within a short amount of time. I guarantee you that by the end of this school year, you are going to feel quite differently about school and about life in general. How does that sound to you?"

How does that sound to me? Unbelievable, if you want to know the truth. The total mess that was my life can change in just three months? And there is actually a name for what is happening with me? Other people have this problem too? I am much luckier than many people with this problem because I am so young? It is a lot to take in. I don't know what to say.

"I am sure this all seems quite overwhelming," Dr. Ogden continues. "Don't worry, your parents and I have developed what I think is a great plan for the next couple of weeks. You have already started taking some medications, and within another week or so they will help you start to feel more in control. We all think that it would be a great idea for you to stay here for the next two weeks. We have a lot of programs here that I know can help you. Ellen will keep working with you, and you'll also get to work with some other staff to learn all kinds of skills that will help you to feel much better about things when you leave here and go back to school. I am sure it seems kind of scary to stay here for that long, but your parents and Ellen and I all think it is the best plan for you."

I nod, not really knowing how else to react to this news. I have really mixed feelings about spending three weeks in the hospital. I do feel safe here, but sooner or later I will have to leave and go back to school. What will I say to explain my absence? What will my classmates say if they find out I have a mental health disorder? It seems to me that will be just more ammunition and make me even more of a target for bullying.

I can hear them in my mind. *Sarah is crazy.* But for now, that's at least two weeks away. For now, I will try not to think about any of that. For now, I will just enjoy walking outside in the sunshine with Mom and Dad, catching up on family news, and eating the ice-cream they buy for me from the cafeteria.

We spend most of the day together. My grandmother is driving my brothers to their sports games in Tardis today and will be making them dinner later, so Mom and Dad stay and eat dinner with me. We talk, we play a board game in the lounge, we watch some television together in my room, and we drink soda. All very normal things, and after they have left and I am sitting on my bed hugging Shelley, I realize the irony of my situation. I am a patient in a mental health ward, and I have been diagnosed with a mental health disorder, yet, for the first time in a very long time, I am beginning to think that my life can perhaps, one day, be normal.

Routine.
Life on the ward
is full of routine.
Wake up to the sound of
"checks."
Name checked off
the list on the clipboard.
Every fifteen minutes.
Am I safe?

Routine.
Breakfast.
"Checks."

Speak to the doctor.
"Checks."

Meet with groups.
"Checks."
Learning coping skills

for when I go back to my life.

How do I work to re-establish friendships?

"Checks."

Learning about mental health issues.

"Checks."

Routine.

I love organization

and routine.

It makes me feel safe.

I know what is coming next.

"Checks."

Safe.

Routine.

After lunch

making things

in the craft room.

Painted bird house.

Threading beads

is therapeutic.

"Checks."

Visitors

from the emotional support dogs program.

Penelope,

Long-haired poodle.

So soothing to

snuggle with her.

She gives me kisses.

Looking forward to her next visit.

She's coming back next week.

It feels as though it's been a long time

since I looked forward to something.

We've talked about getting

a family dog.

I wonder if it will ever happen.

Routine.

"Checks."

Safe.

I am safe here.

It's dinner-time.

"Checks."

Now I have to leave my room
and eat with others.
They place my tray on the table.
Make conversation with those around you.
No tray moving!
Stomach in knots again,
but I will try.
We talk about the food,
the chicken nuggets are delicious.
Eat those first
so we can get to that chocolate cake.
So much frosting.
That's my favorite part too.
It was nice talking to you.
Sleep well.
"Checks."

Medication.
No, it doesn't mean you are crazy.
Yes, soon you will start to feel the effects.
It will help you think clearly.
Medication,
then bed.

Another day of feeling
safe.
Some time to watch television
before I turn off the light.
The noises in the hallway
no longer bothering me.
I am used to it all now.
Safe.

NINETEEN

I AM SURPRISED WHEN I walk into Ellen's office this morning to see Mrs. Shelby sitting there. I have been in the hospital for nearly three weeks, and to be honest, I have almost stopped thinking about school and life outside of the ward. Seeing Mrs. Shelby is a shock, a jolt back to reality. I cannot stay here forever. For a while I have been a mermaid. I have been able to swim away to another part of the ocean. I have lived a very different life. I have cried my mermaid tears, without the need to hide them. But suddenly I can feel the water draining from my ocean. Soon I will be forced to become a girl again.

"It's lovely to see you, Sarah," Mrs. Shelby tells me as I sit down. "I have heard that you have been doing really well here, and that you are nearly ready to come back to school. I spoke with Mr. Douglas this morning before I came here, and he asked me to tell you that he has missed you and is looking forward to having you back in class soon."

"Sarah," Ellen says softly, "Mrs. Shelby has accepted my invitation to come here today so we can all talk about how to make your return to school as easy for you as possible. We both want you to be able to transition back into your regular life in a way that will not be too stressful for you."

I look from one to the other. I hug Shelley to me even closer. I take a deep breath, trying not to panic as the ocean continues to seep away, and I find myself exposed to the air. Don't let the water take your safety away with it, I tell myself. You have been safe here. You can be safe out there.

I listen as Ellen and Mrs. Shelby talk about the plan to release me from the hospital in a few days and have me return to school a few days after that. Mrs. Shelby tells Ellen that she thinks she might go and speak to my class at homeroom time before I go back and prepare them for my return. Ellen says she thinks that is a great idea, and they talk for a while about what Mrs. Shelby will say and what questions she can expect my classmates to ask. What a terrifying thought, to be talked about at school like that. To be so totally exposed before my classmates. I might as well go to school naked.

But the more I think about it, the more I realize that it is actually a good idea. If Mrs. Shelby doesn't say anything, I will be getting endless comments, questions, and speculation. Where have I been? Why have I been in the hospital for three weeks? Is it true that I am crazy? The thought of going back to school is terrifying, but I know I have to do it. The only alternative would be for my family to pack up and move to another town, and I know that's not going to happen! We are not suddenly going to all become mermaids, swim to a new ocean, and start to live different lives.

"How do you feel about all of this?" Ellen asks me when they have finished working out their plan. I tell them how scared I am feeling, and they both nod at me. I know they understand. I have already explained to Ellen about how I sometimes wish I were a mermaid, and we have talked a lot about why I find mermaids so fascinating. I have explained to her about mermaid tears and my soda bottle collection. We have talked about why I feel that it is important to solve the mystery about what would make a mermaid cry, when it seems to me as though their lives would be full of beauty and tranquility.

I remember she asked me if I really thought that sorrow was the only reason for crying. There are so many emotions people feel, she explained, that could make you cry. I discover that tears are streaming down my face, and I am confused. I didn't realize I was crying. Why am I crying? They are both looking at me, waiting for me to speak.

Dr. Ogden explained to me that just because I am now taking medication, learning about my mental health, and developing skills in the groups I've been attending here in the hospital and by talking with Ellen, none of these things are going to work like magic. Like any other illness, he explained, it would take some time for the symptoms to be manageable, but it was going to be possible for me to deal with them and take control.

"Imagine a spiral staircase," he told me. "Make it as beautiful and as ornate as your imagination can conjure up. It is so beautiful that you want to climb it, to see where it leads. You are at the bottom of the staircase. It's quite dark down there. And cold. And lonely. You don't want to stay down there, so you start to climb."

I remember how he stopped and looked at me for a moment to be sure I was following the image he was creating for me.

"Did I forget to say that it is a magical staircase? As you climb, it doesn't sap your energy, make your legs ache, or make you want to stop climbing. As you climb, you get stronger and more determined to reach the top. But there's another strange thing that happens as you climb too. As you go around the spirals in the staircase, you'll find that you come across some familiar things. You might feel yourself feeling down. Or full of too much energy. Or wanting to sleep all day. Or not wanting to sleep at all. Or having difficulty controlling your temper. Or not being able to focus on your school-work. All of the things you have told me about. All of the things that have made your life so difficult for you in the last few years. But as you climb up, you get stronger and stronger, and you'll find that these things will matter less and less. Eventually you will be so strong that none of it will matter. You will be in complete control, and you'll be the person making decisions about who and what you want to be. No-one else. And nothing else."

I fix the image of the spiral staircase firmly in my mind as I look at Ellen and Mrs. Shelby. "I can do this," I whisper finally.

Life is like sea glass.

Some parts are smooth.

Easy to navigate through.

Some parts are sharper.

Once they have touched you,

you can be permanently damaged.

Will I be one of the lucky ones?

The sea glass

has touched me.

There have been many sharp pieces.

They have tried their very best

to slow me down.

To break me.

Will I be strong enough

to heal the wounds?

To resist forming scars?

TWENTY

TODAY IS WEDNESDAY, AND I am going home from the hospital. My mother has taken three days off school to stay with me. We have lots of things to figure out. The first is going to meet my new therapist.

The hospital has arranged for me to work with a lady called Stephanie once a week, starting today. We drive to her office on the way home from the hospital. As we walk in, she smiles and shakes hands with my mother and me. I ask her if she minds that I have brought Shelley in with me, and she laughs. "Of course not," she tells me. "You might be surprised by how many of my clients, of all ages, like to bring a friend like Shelley with them. Come on in, all three of you."

Her office is not at all like either Ellen's or Dr. Ogden's, where I have spent so much time over the last three and a half weeks. Another change to get used to. Stephanie has an assortment of mismatched but very comfortable look-ing chairs, each of which has an oversized cushion and a blanket on it. "You choose where you would like to sit," she tells me. I sit in a big red armchair and rearrange the cushion behind me until I feel comfortable.

"Sometimes I find my clients like to wrap up in a blanket," she tells me. "You and Shelley are welcome to use it anytime you want to," she adds.

It isn't a cold day, and it is definitely not cold in her office, but the idea of being wrapped up in a blanket does sound nice, so I take it off the back of the chair and spread it over Shelley and me. I'm right. It does feel nice. I can see why Stephanie has blankets on every chair.

I'm really glad that the hospital has sent her a complete file of me and everything we talked about there. The thought of having to go over everything again from the beginning is not at all appealing. Ellen told me that this first visit with Stephanie would be for us to get to know each other and that we would meet every week for a while. How long? I wanted to know. Ellen explained that she could not answer that question. It is different for everyone, and Stephanie, my parents, and I will decide that together. Stephanie will meet with the whole family sometimes, including my brothers; sometimes my parents and me; and sometimes just me. We will all have a lot of work to do to learn how to have the best family relationships we can possibly have. We are very lucky, Ellen told me. This is going to be a great experience for our whole family, and we will all have a much stronger relationship and family life because of it. She also told us that we are doubly lucky because Stephanie is one of the best therapists she knows of who specializes in working with families. This is actually a great gift that I am giving to my family.

It is still pretty hard to think of myself as a gift of any kind. I know I put a huge amount of stress on my family, especially my parents. I was in so much pain myself, and I passed a huge amount of that pain onto others in my life. While I always knew that I could not cure my own pain by causing pain to others, I was powerless to stop myself. But here I am, just a few short weeks later, and I recognize that I am beginning to look at things differently.

I can feel that I am beginning to feel more in control of my mind and my body. It is a good feeling. I am beginning to understand that everything I have been through was not my fault. Bipolar disorder is not preventable, or curable, but it is treatable. It is not because of anything I have done or not done. In fact, Dr. Ogden explained that this often runs in families, and he asked both of my parents a lot of questions about their family backgrounds.

We talk for just a short time that first day. My mother and Stephanie spend the rest of our time together working out a schedule for our future appointments. A little bit of guilt does creep back in when I hear that my Dad will have to take some time off work to join us when it is time for our family sessions. Mom assures me he will not mind, that he will think it is time very well spent. I hope she is right. Dad works very hard and is successful at his job. I know that Mom has a reputation for being a great kindergarten teacher too. I think that was what had made me feel so bad for being such a failure and letting them down so badly. But after all the work of the last three weeks, I am starting to believe them when they tell me I have not let them down in any way at all. In fact, they tell me again, the opposite is true. They have let me down by not realizing I needed help.

As we leave Stephanie's office, Mom takes my hand and gives it a squeeze. She smiles at me.

"Everything is going to be okay," she whispers to me. "I promise."

We arrive home to delicious smells wafting out of the kitchen. My grandmother is there, as usual, but instead of just supervising my brothers, she has decided to prepare dinner.

"I thought you might be too tired to cook," she tells my mother. "Welcome home, Sarah. I've missed you." I throw my arms around my grandmother and kiss her. I have missed her too. I haven't seen her since going to the hospital. She has been looking after my brothers while my parents were visiting me, and the hospital's policy restricted visitors to parents only.

"Thank you for Shelley. I love her." I kiss her again. I cry. I hug her, and I cry some more. They are definitely happy tears. I am so happy to see my grandmother. I am happy to be home. Back in my own part of the ocean. And I am happy to see my brothers, who are standing in the kitchen rather awkwardly, as if they don't know what to say to me.

I think my grandmother can sense the awkwardness, so she quickly adds, "Let's get ready for dinner. And if you all clear your plates," she says, looking around at all of us, including my parents, "I have made my famous-in-your-house brownies for dessert. Remember, though, vegetables gone before brownies come out!"

She laughs, and my brothers both groan. They are both famous-in-our-house for their dislike of vegetables. When we had our discussions about the possibility of getting a dog, Adam suggested that we would need to make sure we chose one who loved vegetables so he could sneak his vegetables off his plate and onto the floor and my mother would never know. Ha! Maybe that might have worked if he hadn't told us all his plan well in advance!

My father takes my bag upstairs, and we all sit down at the dining table to enjoy my grandmother's cooking. Fortunately, she has made the whole meal with things she found in our fridge and freezer. When we used to visit her in her old house, she sometimes would serve us weird things for dinner, like cow tongue! My brothers and I thought it was gross, but Mom and Dad both loved it, and would remind us with a glare in our direction that we were expected to eat everything on our plates. So, no tongue today, just chicken, baked potatoes (with lots of butter), and corn on the cob (with even more butter). Nothing to challenge the "eat your vegetables before you can have dessert" rule for either of my brothers.

After dinner, Dad tells my brothers that they will be helping him clean up and do the dishes. They can buy their lunches at school tomorrow, so no need to make sandwiches. My grandmother kisses us all and heads for home, which leaves me and Mom to unpack my things and sort out laundry. When we have finished, Mom sits on my bed and taps the spot beside her. I go over and sit down.

"Sarah," she says, "I know it is not going to be the easiest thing in the world to go back to school, but we have a couple of days to settle in here first. I want you to know that you can share anything with me, anything at all. If you are worried about something, or if there's any help you need. Anything. Okay?"

She sounds uncertain, hoping I will accept her offer of help but not sure if I actually will. I hug her. "Thanks, Mom," is all I say, and I hope it is enough.

TWENTY ONE

MY MOTHER AND I SPEND a lot of time in my room over the next two days. She tells me that one of the things she has decided, while I have been in the hospital, is that my room should reflect me and my interests more. Dad has agreed to turn a blind eye to the fact that we are planning on ignoring his "no pins in the wall" rule. I would never have asked, but Mom says she feels strongly that I should be able to hang up a poster that I made in the hospital. It is my "Important Things" project, and I worked really hard on it, so I am excited that I am going to be able to hang it up, as the therapist suggested. We even take it to Staples first to get it laminated.

I was only in the hospital a few days when we started the poster project. One of the therapists spoke to us all about how important it is to stay focused on the things that we feel strongly about, the things that are important in our lives. We were each given a large sheet of poster paper, and in the middle of the table were markers, glue sticks, and an enormous pile of magazines. The instructions were to create our poster in any way we liked. I think we all started by looking through the magazines.

I started collecting pictures of flowers, books, dogs, Christmas decorations, and some beach scenes. I wasn't surprised to not find any mermaids in the magazines, but that was no problem, I thought. I would just draw some. The staff were very careful with the scissors. We had to ask for a pair, use them, and give them straight back. Slowly but surely, my poster began to reflect the things that are important to me. As I worked on this project, I remember being amazed that there are so many things I care about.

When Mom and I finish arranging things in my room, including giving Shelley a special place to sit on the mermaid blanket on my bed, we talk about where would be the best place to hang my Important Things. Eventually we choose a place right beside my bed, so it will be the last thing I see each night as I get into bed and the first thing I see each morning as I get up. I don't think I will move the furniture around in my room any-more now, because I want my Important Things to always be right next to my bed. And I don't want to push Dad's no pins rule too far! Then Mom has even more exciting news.

"Sarah, I want you to pick out some of your favorite mermaid drawings. We are going to hang those up too." I look around my room once we are finished with our makeover. I am swimming back to my own ocean. I feel safe here. Atargatis had a beautiful temple dedicated to her. It was made of gold and decorated with diamonds. Looking around my room, I think about how I am sure that her temple could not possibly have been more beautiful than my bedroom.

On Friday, Mom suggests lunch at the mall, followed by a manicure and pedicure. I've never had a manicure or a pedicure before, so I am happy to agree. "After all," Mom reminds me, "we still have a birthday to celebrate." To be honest, I had actually forgotten that this whole strange new life began on my birthday, preventing the family barbecue we had planned for that weekend. So, over lunch, we discuss how we should celebrate my birthday. We could have a special family weekend, she tells me, or anything else I want to do.

I don't need any time to think about it. Even though it is early to be thinking about the Cape, I want to make a day trip to Dennis. I want to take a picnic lunch to the beach (with some orange soda from the Mercantile we could pick up on the way), spend some time on the sand, and have dinner at Kreme 'N' Kone on the way home.

"Sounds fantastic!" Mom sounds really enthusiastic about my plan. After all, the whole family loves our time in Dennis every year. "An extra day there will be a celebration for us all," she adds.

So that's how we spend Saturday. Mom packs egg salad sandwiches for our beach picnic. She knows those are my favorite. We stop at the Mercantile, and Mom gives each of us money for soda and a quarter to me for the nickelodeon. I take a quick look around the store, but I don't want to spend too long here. As much as I love the Mercantile, I know we will be back in the summer. For this birthday celebration, I want to spend as much time as possible at the beach. I choose my usual orange soda, and my brothers get their favorite, root beer. We get a four-pack each! Mom and Dad both say they will stick with coffee. On our way to the beach, we stop to get a big bag of ice so we can enjoy our soda cold while we are at the beach.

Although it's a little cold because it's early in the season, it doesn't matter to me at all. I just wear my sweatshirt as I go through my usual routines. Treasure collecting. Treasure sorting. I find some really pretty shells to start my new collection. Mom and I found a special spot in my made-over bedroom, and she has given me a brand-new glass jar to restart my collection. No mermaid tears to-day, though. Maybe when we come back in the summer.

My brothers spend their time building complex sand-castle structures, complete with moats. Mom and Dad seem to enjoy just relaxing with their coffee. I see them watching all three of us kids and smiling to each other a lot.

I didn't bring a book today, so after the treasure collecting is done, we all take a long walk along the beach. We wade a bit in the ocean, squealing when a particularly cold wave wraps around our ankles. All too soon, it is time to leave, but there is still Kreme 'N Kone to enjoy on the way home. I briefly consider ordering something different, and even study the menu for several minutes. But eventually I go for my usual broiled sea scallops with rice pilaf and coleslaw. Delicious. As we leave, we buy our soft-serve dessert and set off for home.

As we drive home, I try really hard to focus on the day and not think about what is going to happen in just one more day. It has been a really good day. Don't think about Monday, I tell myself. Just focus on today, and think about how lucky you are to have had an extra Dennis day. It has been a really good day. Focus on putting your new treasures into your brand-new jar when you get home. It has been a really good day.

TWENTY TWO

WE TALK A LOT ABOUT it on Sunday, and before I know it, Monday has arrived. Back to school. I am incredibly nervous, but I believed Mrs. Shelby when she told me, back in that hospital meeting, that she would help me to make my return as smooth as possible. I eat my breakfast, grab my backpack, and walk outside to wait for the bus. My mother suggested that she could drive me to school today, but I think it will be better if I get straight back into the usual routine. I can feel her watching me from the kitchen window, so I try very hard to look relaxed and confident. But when the bus appears around the corner of my street, I am not feeling relaxed or confident at all.

I climb onto the bus and take a seat in the front row, feeling as though all eyes are on me. It seems unusually quiet for a Monday morning, but once the bus starts moving again the conversation resumes. I notice that when the bus stops to add passengers between my house and school, the conversation decibels do not lower at all. I'm not surprised.

I know I am the focus of some stares as I walk into the building and head down the hallway toward homeroom. I am anxious to get there. Not only will it get me out of the hallway, but I will be glad to see Mr. Douglas. When I arrive at Room 7, he is standing in the doorway, waiting to greet me.

"Welcome back, Sarah. Come on in, and let's get you organized." We head over to my desk, where I empty my backpack and try to ignore everyone else in the room. My parents and I have already agreed that I will attend summer school part-time to help me catch up on the curriculum I have missed in my nearly one month away, so I'm not worried about how behind I will be. What I am worried about is how I am going to answer what I think will be the inevitable questions about where I have been.

Mrs. Shelby told me she would be talking with the class, but she didn't tell me what she was going to say, so I really don't know what to expect. Once I have my binder, books, and pencil pouch organized on my desk, I head out to my locker to deposit my bag and jacket. Giuseppe and I meet in the doorway.

"Sarah! Hi, I'm glad you are back!" He seems genuinely pleased to see me. "I'm looking forward to catching up with you at lunch today. No-one else seems to appreciate me wanting to talk about books while we eat." He laughs.

He has told me many times that it frustrates him that sixth grade boys only ever seem to want to talk about sports at lunch.

I smile at him. "I missed you too, Giuseppe. I'm glad to be back." As soon as those words are out of my mouth, I realize that I actually mean them. I have missed Giuseppe. He has become a good friend, and being away has helped me to recognize that. But even more than that, I am glad to be back at school. I am a little bit surprised to realize this is true. I think about that spiral staircase. I'm climbing. I'm getting stronger. I'm swimming back to my home waters, and for the first time in a very long time, I think that perhaps I can actually cope.

Dr. Ogden was quite clear in our conversations. There are no magical cures, and no easy solutions, to anything that happened in my life over the past couple of years. Bipolar disorder has no cure. But he also made sure I understood that the symptoms could be managed very well, and he told me many times that I was very lucky to have been diagnosed early. He told me there is a very high success rate with people who are diagnosed at my age and that they are able to live completely normal lives. It's not going to be easy, though, he told me. There will be a lot of hard work involved.

That hard work begins on my first day back at school. I have already talked a lot with both Ellen and Stephanie about how to deal with the inevitable questions, any future bullying, and all of those other relationship issues that made my life so difficult in the past. From day one, I have to put these new skills into practice, but I am definitely feeling a little stronger. I know I have a backup plan (go to the guidance office any-time I need to), and I know I can tell Mr. Douglas at any time that I need to talk to him, and he will find time for me during the day. I'm climbing the spiral staircase.

I am so glad that Mondays begin with ELA, followed by social studies. The class began new book studies while I was gone, so Mr. Douglas shows me the book choices and tells me I can take some time to decide which group I would like to join. They all look good, so once I have made my choice, I take out my folder and add the other titles to my "Books I Want to Read" list. I spend the rest of the time reading. I can join in the book discussions, Mr. Douglas tells me, once I have caught up with the group. I know that won't take me long, since I love reading, and the groups have only been working for a few days on these projects.

Social studies is a little more challenging. While I have been away, the class has finished their historical studies and begun a unit on government. I have missed the end-of-unit assessment for the history of Massachusetts, but Mr. Douglas tells me not to be concerned about this. He has some notes for me covering the parts of the topic I have missed, and when I have settled back into the school routine, he has an idea for a project I can do to make up for the missing grade. He even has some notes for me covering the beginnings of the government unit. I can see he has put a lot of time and effort into preparing all this for me, and I am very grateful.

Health and physical education are next, and I find myself with very mixed feelings as I walk down the hallway toward the classroom and Mrs. Paul. After the incident in her class, I am not at all sure how to face her, or Shannon, despite all the talking I have done with Ellen and Stephanie. We begin in the gym, and, thankfully, we are not doing a team activity today. It is fitness circuit time, which I would normally hate, but I know I can move around the stations at my own speed, and I do my best to ignore others around me. Shannon is there, of course, along with all of the others who were there "that day."

The others in the class all seem very familiar with the activities at each station. They barely even glance at the instruction cards as they move around the circuit, exercising in all of the required different ways. Of course, it is all new to me, so I study the instruction cards carefully each time Mrs. Paul blows the whistle and we move clockwise around the gym. I know she is watching me, and after the first couple of station changes, she comes over and whispers to me,

"Sarah, I'm glad you are back in class, but I'd like to see you doing a little more than just reading the instruction cards, please." She smiles in that knowing way teachers have. I thought my tactic to avoid getting too physical was working. I nod, pick up a jump rope, and start following the directions on the card.

In health, the class has been divided into groups, with each group working on a presentation on alcohol, tobacco, and other drugs. The research phase is already completed, so everyone is working on how they will share their findings with the rest of the class. Mrs. Paul asks me if I have any preference for which group I join. I really don't, although I had hoped to avoid working with Shannon so soon after the last time we were in the same group. I join the group working on the effects of secondhand smoke. They are working on a presentation using Google slides, so I ask how they would like me to help.

"We're nearly done," Jason replies. "We've worked really hard on this, so I hope you are not going to end up with the same grade as the rest of us, considering you'll have done almost nothing toward it." The other group members don't say anything, but I can tell by the looks on their faces that they agree with Jason's opinion. I have to admit, I can see their point of view. I'm not concerned about grades at all, since I already know I will be going to summer school, but they don't know that. The much bigger issue for me is settling back into each class, and trying my very best to have positive interactions with my classmates.

"I don't know what Mrs. Paul will do," I tell them, "but I'm sure she will be fair to everyone. Can I just help with anything that's left to do?" They tell me I can proof-read the slides that are completed, so I open the nearest Chromebook and get started. I'm climbing that spiral staircase.

Lunch-time is a welcome break. I sit at my usual back table, and Giuseppe and I talk about nothing in particular. I can tell he is trying to avoid any references to the past few weeks, and I'm not ready to bring it up yet with him. Ellen and I have rehearsed these types of situations, but I decide I need to take a few more steps up that spiral staircase before I will be ready to start a conversation like that.

The rest of the day, in fact, the rest of the week, goes along in pretty much the same way. I do go down to the guidance office a couple of times. But it is actually not a bad week, all things considered. My teachers are all doing their best to ease me back into the workload and to help me catch up on anything I need to know from what I have missed. I am pretty lucky in that. I have missed the whole algebra unit, which I can catch up on during the summer, and the new unit on measurement has just begun. I never thought I would consider myself lucky in anything to do with math!

TWENTY THREE

LOOKING BACK ON OUR CONVERSATIONS, I realize Dr. Ogden was right. About so many things. It has not been easy to return to school, even though I talked about it a lot with Ellen. She reminded me that even though Mrs. Shelby was going to talk to my homeroom, there are many more students in my grade that I have classes with every day. Some of them would ignore me, she told me, as they have done before, but some would probably have a difficult time letting go of their negative impressions. I know my brain explosions affected a lot of people. Family. Friends. Classmates. Teachers. But the one affected most was me. And by helping me, Dr. Ogden has assured me, I will be helping the others too.

So I work hard on helping me. I work hard on continuing to climb that staircase. Every week when I have my appointment with Stephanie, I continue to try very hard to be completely open and honest about things that are happening in my life and how I am feeling. Shelley and

I have started to feel quite comfortable in that big red armchair, wrapped in the blanket, sharing our innermost thoughts.

My mother makes sure I take my medications every day, but I honestly think that even without her watching me, I would be responsible about swallowing them every morning, because I am definitely now beginning to feel their effect on me. I am more in control of my thoughts and my body than I have been in a very long time. I am beginning to feel as though it is safe to shed some of the many masks I have been hiding behind for so long. I am beginning to feel that perhaps I do have something to contribute to my family, and maybe even to my classmates. Giuseppe has been a good friend to me over the past few months. Perhaps I can even make new friends.

The image Dr. Ogden has given me of the spiral staircase is proving to be both helpful and true. It isn't always easy to climb those stairs. In fact, sometimes I think it probably takes me several days, or even more, to climb just one. But I know without a doubt that I am moving in the right direction, and as I climb, I can feel myself getting stronger and better able to deal with the judgments and negative comments of others that still come my way at times because, for many of my classmates, the old Sarah is a very recent memory.

I can't blame them. I hadn't liked myself very much, so how could I have expected others to like me?

So I continue the hard work of climbing those stairs as the end of the school year approaches. Knowing I have the opportunity to attend summer school actually makes things a lot easier academically. I don't need to worry about grades, although I do my best work for every class, as I have always tried to do. The thought of summer school doesn't concern me at all. I am actually looking forward to it. The chance to catch up on anything I have missed, as well as any work I have not understood the first time through, seems like a wonderful gift. Like an extra birthday gift, perhaps. My mother smiles and hugs me when I tell her that is how I feel about it. And summer school will be over by the first week of August, so it will not interfere at all with our family Dennis week.

Today when I arrive home after school, my grandmother delivers the news that after snack time (brownies again!), it will be fine with her if I want to go upstairs to do my homework. I can't even begin to find the words to explain how good that makes me feel. After I have finished all my assignments, I search the bottom of my closet until I find all of my crocheted mermaid supplies.

Adam and Daniel are watching television when I go downstairs, and my grandmother is making herself a cup of coffee. When she sees what I am carrying, she rushes over to me and gives me a huge hug. I can see there are tears in her eyes. There are some in mine too!

"Gran, would you help me get started on my mermaid again, please?" I ask as I start spreading the yarn, pattern, and partly-finished mermaid out on the kitchen counter.

"Oh, sweetheart, I would love to. Nothing would make me happier," she tells me. "I was wondering about suggesting it, but I'm so happy you asked me. You have done such an amazing job with her so far. We can work on her a little bit every day after homework, and if she isn't finished by the end of the school year, we can carry on over the summer."

We sit down together at the kitchen table and resume the project I abandoned months ago.

"What are you going to call her?" Gran asks me.

"Atargatis," I tell her.

Who am I?

How do you define a person?

Is it by what you can see?

Is it by their physical appearance?

Is that who I am?

If so, then I am the girl with blonde hair.

The not very tall girl.

The girl who wears glasses and braces.

Or is it by how a person behaves?

Then I am the quiet girl.

The girl who likes to curl up for hours

with a book.

The girl who spends many hours drawing, creating.

The girl who loves to help other people

and animals.

The girl who still loves her dolls and her bears.

Doesn't care that others say she is too old.

Or is it by how others behave

towards you?

Then I am the girl others are beginning

to understand.

The girl some classmates are reaching out to.

An invitation to hang out at the mall

gratefully received.

And accepted.

Or is it by what is inside a person?

Then I am the thoughtful girl.

The always-try-to-remain-in-control girl.

The calmer,

Beginning-to-trust-others girl.

The people-don't-mean-to-hurt-you girl.

Just let them get to know you.

Friendships are built on

Understanding,

Empathy,

Cooperation.

There's power in letting people in.

A difficult lesson,

but one that is growing within me.

Or maybe
a person shouldn't be defined at all.
Everyone is evolving,
changing,
developing.
I am not who I used to be.
Are you?

People are not
inanimate objects.
To be categorized.
Limited by the perceptions
or expectations
of others.

Who was I born to be?
I realize I don't know that yet.
I have barely begun the journey
to define myself.

My world is filling with water.
But not so I can drown myself.
Or swim away to escape.

Instead, the whole ocean is mine,

to explore,

to enjoy,

to embrace.

So many possibilities.

I will be like Atargatis.

I will not let the past

define my future.

I will journey and discover

until there is nothing left

that is unknown to me.

TWENTY FOUR

GIUSEPPE AND I FIND OUR lunch group growing steadily over these final few weeks of the school year. Michelle is the first to join us. She joins in our book discussions with great enthusiasm. I'm not sure if it is Michelle's bubbly personality, Giuseppe's good looks, or what (maybe even something to do with me), but our group continues to grow until finally the table is at its seating limit. I find myself looking forward to lunch-time and having actual conversations with people I am beginning to think of as friends.

We have moved beyond just talking about books and school-work. It feels like it is a good sign that these lunch friends and I have other things to talk about now. Important things, like what color we should paint our nails (Giuseppe groans at that) and how annoying our parents can be sometimes.

I won't pretend it is always easy. I have been hurt so many times in the past that I am definitely being cautious. Stephanie and I talk a lot about lunch-time, and she helps me to feel more comfortable in opening myself up more to my tablemates. I am feeling much safer now letting people see inside me. Occasionally I still feel that sense of panic, and for a moment I will consider pulling on a mask. But the more Stephanie and I talk about it, and the more I practice doing it, having real conversations is becoming easier and easier.

I think it was Michelle's invitation to hang out with her at the mall last Saturday that was a turning point for me. I tell myself that she would not have done that if she didn't really want to spend time with me. People can fake it at school. They can be sitting with me because either Mr. Douglas or one of the other teachers has suggested it would be a good thing to do. But to choose to invite me to spend time with her on the weekend is something else entirely, and it takes me several steps up the spiral staircase.

We had a great time at the mall. Michelle's mom dropped us off, and my mom picked us up when I called her and told her we were done. In between those two car trips, we visited every clothing store and looked at the new outfits for the coming summer. We both found several we would like to buy, so we decided it was time to start saving our allowances. It was amazing how long we spent deciding what to eat for lunch in the food court, but eventually we went back to the first thing we thought of. Pizza. While we were eating our pizza, Michelle did something that really surprised me. She told me that she wanted to share something with me. Something that was really troubling her and that she needed some advice about.

As we ate, Michelle shared that she had recently learned that her parents were going to be getting a divorce, because they just could not get along together any longer. Her mother had kicked her father out of the house a few weeks before, and Michelle was feeling really guilty about feeling glad that he was gone. She told me that she did miss her father, and had not seen him since he moved out, but that it was so nice that the arguments and fights that had become normal in her home were now over.

I was a little startled at first. This was something very personal, and I wondered why she was telling me. I guess my face must have revealed my shock, because she quickly added, "I hope you don't mind me telling you this. I just thought you might understand someone having a problem to deal with because, well, you know . . ." She stopped speaking as her cheeks reddened.

"Of course I don't mind," I quickly reassured her. "I've certainly learned recently how important it is to talk about things that are bothering you. But I really don't know what I can do to help."

I was surprised when she told me that I had already helped, just by allowing her to tell someone about it. Michelle is an only child, so it must be strange to just have her mother at home with her now. I shared with her that I understood all about feeling guilty. I told her how helpful Mr. Douglas and Mrs. Shelby had been to me, and I tried really hard to assure her that they could both be trusted to offer good advice. She told me she would think about it. As we talked, I realized that Michelle had a spiral staircase of her own, and that she had just taken some very big steps to begin her climb upwards.

Finally, when we had finished eating and talking, we went into Claire's. Michelle has pierced ears, so she wanted to spend some of the money she had received for her birthday last month on new earrings. While she was choosing from the huge selection, I looked around, and I came up with a great idea. I couldn't wait to talk to my grandmother about it after school on Monday.

TWENTY FIVE

ONE OF THE THINGS I find amazing about my grandmother's MINI Cooper is how much she can fit inside of it. Like the "real" Tardis, she is always saying, "It really is bigger on the inside, you know, Sarah!" Now that she has retired, she spends a lot of time making things. As well as knitting and crocheting blankets and scarves, she also makes beautiful greeting cards, some jewelry (mainly earrings), and a few other things that match the season.

Just before last Christmas, she was sewing Christmas stockings in all kinds of beautiful Christmas fabrics. Every now and then, she puts the back seats down and loads Tardis up to the roof with a pop-up tent, tables, chairs, and all her crafts. Off she goes to sell what she has made at a craft fair. I know she really enjoys making the crafts, and I think she enjoys the fairs just as much. She is always just as excited about telling us about the people she meets there as she is about how much money she has made.

That's where my idea comes in. She has already invited me to come with her to a fair any-time I want to go. Wouldn't it be awesome, I thought, if we both had things to sell? We discuss it, and she agrees to help me make some bracelets. We made bracelets and necklaces in the craft room at the hospital, and I really enjoyed it. I had loved choosing the colors I would put together and deciding on the pattern of beads for each item I made. I kept one of those bracelets and gave the rest away to nurses who had been kind to me.

Gran explains how, when she buys supplies, she uses coupons and sales to make sure she gets the best deals so she can sell her crafts at a good price. She tells me she will help me buy supplies, and we can work on projects together.

Then I have another idea. I know Michelle likes jewelry, from all the time and talking we spent in Claire's the other day. What if I were to invite her over to work on making bracelets, and we could both go to the craft fair? I tell my grandmother all about my visit to the mall on Saturday and about how Michelle has some tough stuff going on at the moment. "I'd really like to help her if I can," I add.

As I expected, my grandmother thinks it is a great idea. Of course, we will have to get Michelle's mom's permission, she reminds me, but I'm pretty sure that won't be a problem. She was so happy to drive us to the mall on

Saturday and seemed really pleased that Michelle and I were becoming friends.

I'm going to finish my crocheted mermaid first. I can't wait to get to the part where I give Atargatis her hair and decide what style to make it. She is going to have long, shimmery purple hair. I am so excited; I just can't wait to get her finished. She will have a special place to sit, beside Shelley, on my mermaid blanket.

I really love my room now that it is such a reflection of who I am. I don't feel trapped there anymore. Instead, I look forward to the time I spend relaxing, being creative, reading, and working on my school projects. Sometimes I do need to step off the staircase for a while and just be still in my room, but most of the time I can feel the progress I am making. For the first time in a very long time, I truly feel as though I am okay being me.

PART FOUR

*"When one man, for whatever reason, has the
opportunity to lead an extraordinary life, he has
no right to keep it to himself."*

- Jacques Cousteau

TWENTY SIX

AS I RELAX ON MAYFLOWER Beach, there are lots of things on my mind. But the thoughts occupying me this year are so very different from the ones I was struggling with last year. I'm thinking about Michelle and Giuseppe and some of the others I have started to consider to be my friends. Once I allowed myself to begin to really open up and let my true self be seen, I found developing these relationships became easier day by day. I am still working weekly with Stephanie. My family is, too, and I know that we are all getting on much better together. So it seems like I have given my family a gift after all. I can truly say that it makes me feel good to think of our visits to Stephanie in that way. I've come to love that big red armchair and the feeling that there is nothing that is off-limits to talk about when I am sitting in it.

Another amazing thing that happened toward the end of the school year was a slow repairing of relationships with some of my friends of the past. I think back over all of those relationships too. Patricia was the first. I will never forget the day she asked me if she could come around one afternoon. I remember feeling very nervous waiting for her arrival, but the visit went well. I had mentioned to my grandmother that she would be coming on the weekend, so the Friday afternoon snack had been a double batch of chocolate chip cookies, which she had remembered were Patricia's favorite. And I will never forget when Patricia walked into my bedroom and spotted Shelley and Atargatis sitting on my bed. The expression of delight on her face was genuine when I told her that I had made Atargatis, with help from my grandmother.

We ate lots of cookies, played lots of card games, and talked about school happenings. She told me that she had continued to go geocaching with her family and that her parents had got quite a few of their friends doing it too. We talked about how it would be fun to ask our parents if we could have our own accounts and perhaps get some of our friends at school to join in too. I have my account now, and I know Patricia does too. I'm going to work on Giuseppe and Michelle when we get back to school. Then I'll see how many others I can add. Patricia and I decided to make a competition out of it. How many can we each get to be involved?

As well, I find myself reflecting on the month I just completed at summer school. What an amazing experience. Summer school was held in the high school, so we got to enjoy air-conditioned comfort. I did have quite a lot of work to catch up on. Work I had missed while I was in the hospital. Work that was so much easier with individual attention from the tutors and no distractions to drag my mind from my assignments.

I was thrilled when Mr. Douglas dropped by one day to see how I was doing. I felt really proud to show him everything I was working on. There was lots of math. Yes, math. And I was proud to share my work!

One of the tutors that I worked with a lot was Ms. Cohen. She was one of the teaching assistants at Michaels Middle during the school year, and she worked part- time at summer school, she explained to me, so she could save up for grad school. Her long-term goal was to be a middle school guidance counselor. Our paths had not crossed at all during the school year, but I'm certainly glad I got to work with her at summer school.

She asked me lots of questions about my studying habits. Because I had always been a good reader, I had assumed that the way to learn new information, like when we were going to have a test, was to read and reread the material.

Ms. Cohen told me about something she had learned in a recent grad school course she had completed.

She explained to me that there is a lot of research to support the idea that there is a strong connection between writing things by hand and that information being retained by your brain. She told me how surprised she and her classmates had been to discover this, since pretty much everyone was using a laptop rather than a notebook to take lecture notes and study for exams. She spent a lot of time with me, practicing how to write notes about what I was trying to learn and then write notes about the notes, summarizing the information more and more as we went along. I couldn't believe none of my teachers had showed me this technique before. Or maybe they had, but I had just not been able to focus for long enough to absorb what they were teaching. Either way, I was glad to know about it now.

I found I was actually enjoying practicing this skill. When I showed my mother what I was doing one afternoon, she took me on a special trip to Staples to buy me some pretty new notebooks. There were so many beautiful cover designs, I remember having a lot of trouble choosing. Mom was so patient, and in the end, we walked out of the store with ten new notebooks and a promise to come back as soon as I needed more.

We are eating our Breakfast Room meal when I notice something going on between Mom and Dad. To be honest, I've actually seen the strange looks they have been giving each other over the whole week, but I just kept telling myself I was imagining it. This morning, it can no longer be denied. Something is going on. I decide to confront it head-on.

"Out with it!" I demand. "You two have been giving each other strange looks all week, and I want to know what is going on." The looks continue back and forth for a moment. Finally, Mom speaks.

"There is going to be a new addition to our family," she explains. That does not explain anything! Is she pregnant? Seriously? Aren't the three of us enough of a challenge? I know she really enjoys working with the kindergarten kids at school, but does she really want another one of her own?

My thoughts must be reflected on my face, because Dad quickly adds, "No! No! No more humans!" Mom starts to laugh.

"A few weeks ago, I saw a picture of a little dog, a Chihuahua, actually, on the town animal shelter Facebook page. I know how much you have wanted a dog, Sarah. When I saw what her shelter name was, I just knew she had to join our family. We are picking her up on the way home," Mom explains. "Her name is Sara, without an '*h*', but you can change that if you would like to. They rescued her a while ago, but she needed surgery on her back legs before she was ready to be adopted. It's been so hard to keep this a secret from you. Dad and I signed the papers before we came here, and they said they will have her ready early this afternoon."

Now I understand the extra rushing and pressure to get the cottage cleaned and packed up this morning. I am so excited that I can't eat another bite!

The drive to the shelter takes days. Weeks. Years. I have so many questions, and Mom patiently answers each one. Sara was rescued about two months ago, from an animal hoarding situation. I don't know what an animal hoarder is, so Mom explains.

Apparently, an animal hoarder usually starts off with good intentions. They want to help animals, and it seems as though the lady who had Sara was like this. But things got out of hand, especially when she got to be too sick to take care of the animals. She had many dogs, all Chihuahuas, who all lived in the basement of her house. No-one had realized how many dogs she had down there until she died and her children came around to clean out the house. They immediately called animal control, and the dogs that were still alive were rescued.

Many of the dogs were quite sick when they were rescued. Some were so sick they didn't make it. Sara wasn't sick, but she couldn't walk. The people at the shelter took her to the vet, who discovered that her back legs had a deformity, which needed surgery. Mom shows me the picture they had posted on the shelter website showing her back legs in plaster after the surgery. Her plaster was bright pink, and she looked so cute, but I am sure the poor thing didn't enjoy having it on her legs. While she recovered from the surgery, she was fostered by a nice lady so that she wouldn't have to stay in the shelter. Now that her plasters are off and she is able to walk on her own, she is ready to go to her own home.

I never get car-sick, but the excitement is building up in me so much that I actually begin to feel quite nauseous and wish I had eaten even less of my breakfast. I try hard to calm my stomach and focus on the picture Mom showed me of little Sara. Finally, Dad turns the car into the driveway of the animal shelter, and I know a wonderful new adventure is about to begin.

TWENTY SEVEN

CYNDI. HER NAME IS CYNDI. She only weighs five pounds, but every ounce of those five pounds is full of sweetness, curiosity, and fear. I can't even imagine what her previous life was like, but I have promised her that I will never let anything bad happen to her ever again. I remind her of that promise every day.

I can tell that I am going to have to work very hard to earn her trust. There are so many things she is afraid of. I guess she and I have some things in common. We both have some issues to work on, but it's okay, because we can work on them together.

Although Cyndi is a member of the whole family, Mom and Dad told me that I am really her mother. They will pay the bills, but I am the one responsible for taking care of her and making sure she is fed, exercised, and happy. We have had pets in our family before. Goldfish. Lots of gold-fish. They never seemed to live very long, and eventually they were all buried under the apple tree at the far end of the garden. Cyndi is different. I don't think of her as a pet. She is part of the family.

I really don't know how they managed to pull it off, but when we first arrived home from the Cape and the shelter, I discovered that Mom and Dad had been planning and preparing for Cyndi's arrival for a while. They had bought beds, blankets, food, bowls, potty pads, and an assortment of toys, and had successfully kept them concealed so the big secret would not leak out. I have to say, I was impressed with their deviousness.

Cyndi lived her previous life in the basement of a house, on a concrete floor, with no heat, very little light, and probably not enough food. She may have even been born down there and had definitely had a number of litters of puppies herself. All of this while being unable to walk. When she was rescued, she could only get around the basement by dragging her rear end along. She had experienced very little human contact and had so much to learn about how kind humans can be. It breaks my heart to think about it, but at the same time, I feel excited at the thought of what she and I can learn and achieve together.

I'll be going into seventh grade next year. I am sure that will bring more challenges. New teachers to get used to. I know I am going to miss seeing Mr. Douglas every day, although I know I will see him in the building. He told me at the end of last year, and reminded me at summer school, to be sure that I come visit him regularly and let him know how things are going.

There will be new classmates to get used to. Classes are shuffled up each year, so I know I will be in the same classes as some of the kids I worked with last year, but there will be lots of new ones too. At least we are all together still for lunch, so Giuseppe, Michelle, and the rest of our group will still be able to spend time together each day. Even if we don't get to spend much time together during the school day, Giuseppe, Michelle, and I have promised each other that we will find time to do things together.

I'm actually getting quite excited about the new school year. I am absolutely determined that I am going to get some Bs on my first report card. I know I can do it. I learned so much about my own learning style at summer school, and I can't wait to show my teachers the new, improved academic version of Sarah!

Another thing I am looking forward to in seventh grade is being a library assistant. Our school librarian, Mr. Lucas, lets kids who want to help out in the library sign up to be a student library assistant. They come in before school three days a week and help out with tasks like cleaning, shelving, and making displays, as well as coming up with ideas for programs for the library. Last year, the assistants organized several book auctions, where donated books were auctioned off for minutes of service to the library. Those were really popular events. Signing up was Mr. Douglas's idea. I hadn't thought about it before, even though I knew the group existed. I think it will be a fun way to start the day, and I'll get to talk to Mr. Lucas about the new books that come in. I can hardly wait!

Don't get me wrong. That spiral staircase is still there. I'm nowhere near the top of it, and I know that I have a huge amount of climbing still to do. Cyndi has one, too, and we are going to climb together. Cyndi and I have talked a lot about this, and we have realized something very important. I used to be so focused on what was going wrong in my own life that I didn't realize that I was not the only one with problems. Watching Cyndi's struggles and talking with Stephanie about everything to do with Cyndi and with me has made me recognize the fact that everyone has something that they are dealing with.

I remember when I found out last year about Giuseppe and his family moving to our town after losing their home following a flood. I was really surprised when I found this out, because Giuseppe always seems to be so cheerful and, well, normal. That must have been a really difficult experience to live through, and adjusting to winter in New England couldn't have helped much. Now I visualize him climbing his own staircase, and I understand why he always seems uncomfortable when the weather is particularly stormy.

I'm not so different after all. Everyone has their own spiral staircase, even if they don't know it. I'm actually one of the lucky ones. I've found my staircase. I'm on my way up, and I know how to find the strength to keep climbing.

I used to wish I was normal, but now I realize there is no such thing. I know that some people are still going to judge me and others who have a mental illness. Or a physical illness. Or live in a different place. Or have different-colored skin. Or any one of those millions of ways we can be different from each other. Too bad. Cyndi and I don't care about judgments. No, a puppy would not be better. Someone who has been damaged by life really can bounce back. Cyndi and I are going to prove that. World, here we come!

The truth

about me

is messy

and

complicated.

But the truth about me

is that I am not

any of the labels

others have given me.

Or any of the labels

I have given myself.

I longed to be

normal.

To be like

everyone else.

Normal.

You have no meaning to me now.

Normal.

You have no power over me now.

I am me.

No explanation needed.

My dad got hepatitis.

He needed medicine.

My uncle has diabetes.

He needs medicine.

I have bipolar disorder.

I need medicine.

But not to make me

normal.

To make me able to be

ME.

Me

has no reason for guilt.

Me

has not disappointed my parents.

They do not need
what I thought they needed.
They do not need
a well-behaved
and academically successful
daughter.
They need a daughter
who is happy
with herself
and her life.
Inside me were
Guilt.
Fears.
Dark thoughts.
Guilt caused me to want to
hide from the whole world.
Now I want to
embrace it.
To live life.
To discover
who I really am.

I have the power

and the tools I need

to discover

ME.

I know now

why mermaids cry.

ACKNOWLEDGEMENTS

THERE ARE MANY PEOPLE I would like to thank for the role they have played in the telling of Sarah's story. Mr. Douglas, thank you for your support, suggestions, and encouragement. Thank you most of all for being "Mr. Douglas" to so many, of all ages, over the years. Special thanks to the real characters in my own life who have inspired Sarah's important people. Your contributions to Sarah's story, and to my own, are valued and appreciated.

Special thanks go to the designer of the beautiful cover, Andrea (our Parker connection makes this extra special for me), and to Jennifer, for all of her help with editing Sarah's story and for all that I have learned from her. And, of course, thanks to Tim of Izzard Ink for his assistance and guidance in the making of Sarah's story a reality.

There are also two organizations I would like to mention because they have had such a profound influence on the development of the person that is Susan L. Read. The Medfield Animal Shelter, in Medfield, Massachusetts, is the shelter that rescued the real-life Cyndi, giving her the shelter name Sara, the surgery she so desperately needed, and is continuing to work daily to rescue and rehome animals in need. National Mill Dog Rescue, based in Peyton, Colorado, has to date rescued over 15,000 dogs that were considered discards from the puppy mill breeding industry. These dogs all have a second chance at life in families of their own. Without NMDR, these dogs would all have been killed. The story of one of the 15,000, Poppy, will be featured in the next book in the Michaels Middle School series.

CPSIA information can be obtained
at www.ICGtesting.com
Printed in the USA
LVHW111441090123
736766LV00020B/164